Last Mom Standing

Mary Jane Owen

Pepperback Press, Inc.

1

Friday Afternoon

"Well, that's not right," I muttered to myself, doing a double take at the image on my screen. Whoever had worked on this file last had somehow changed the company logo from traffic cone orange to fire truck red. I wasn't a fan of the orange, honestly, but the client is always right.

Or whatever.

I was rifling through the papers on my desk to find the sticky note with the hex code of the right color on it when something banged against the old french doors beside me. I jumped and swiveled to find myself in a staring contest with a fat brown chicken.

I blinked.

It didn't.

Instead the chicken banged its pointy face against the wavy glass again, beady eyes examining the moving boxes strewn across my office with an air of judgment.

God, I missed the city.

"There are chickens in the backyard!" Hillary stuck her head into the office, frizzy white blonde curls flying every which way. "I'm going to catch one!"

She was gone again before I could reply, door slamming behind her with enough force to rattle my teeth. I dropped my head into my hands and wondered, not for the first time, if moving my daughters to a dilapidated Victorian farmhouse in the mountains of Virginia was really the best manifestation of my post-divorce midlife crisis.

"I should have just bought a sports car and had a brief but super hot affair with a gym bro," I muttered to my empty office. The chicken peered in again, tilting its head as if to say 'too late now, city girl.'

This cluttered space was a far cry from my sleek corner office in downtown DC, but it definitely had charm. I loved the french doors and the big windows and I was trying really hard to ignore the several layers of lumpy paint on the trim and the wallpaper peeling like an onion above the chair rail.

The anxiety of knowing I needed to strip one hundred years of the previous owners' bad decorating choices was a low level buzz at the back of my brain.

Ah, the joys of home ownership.

A shriek from the backyard made me jump again and I shut my laptop with a little more force than necessary.

"Time to call it a day," I announced firmly to the cluttered room and sent up a sigh of thanks that it was Friday. It had been a really long week. Maybe I'd try to finish unpacking the office later tonight, but for now, I was done. There was no point in trying to work when Hillary was in full feral eight-year-old mode.

I made my way to the living room where the television was droning in front of the big empty couch.

"...increased rates of a new strain of viral pneumonia caused by a Gram-Negative infection, known as a GRM. Officials in Richmond and the surrounding counties are strongly recommending..."

I turned it off. Just what we didn't need—another new virus of the week.

Hands on my hips, I scanned the room. At least it was box free and looking somewhat put together. The couch had been better suited to our Georgetown brownstone. It was a little too big and a little too modern for this house, but the room was warm and cozy with the large fireplace taking center stage, opposite more of those gorgeous large windows.

I carefully avoided looking at the peeling paint on the ornate mantel as the smell of garlic and butter drew me through the room and into the large country kitchen. Frances stood in front of the antique stove, stirring something that smelled divine.

My stomach growled hopefully.

"Smells amazing, honey. Sharing is caring?"

My eldest daughter gave me a look that promised death. "No." She switched off the burner and swept past me with her plate, leaving me alone in the kitchen.

"You could always order in," she called over her shoulder, voice dripping with the level of sarcasm only a seventeen-year-old girl could achieve. "Oh wait, I forgot. There's no delivery in this barren wasteland."

I sighed and opened the fridge, ignoring the familiar pang of guilt. "Technically, this area is quite fertile," I muttered. "It's literally farmland."

Unlike Hillary, Frances was still firmly Team City Life—and sometimes it felt like Team Dad, despite his dramatic departure from our lives with his twenty-something secretary.

Some clichés existed for a reason.

Another screech from outside made me close my eyes and count to ten. "Hillary! Stop tormenting the local wildlife!"

"It's not wildlife, Mom! It's dinner!" came the faint reply.

"It absolutely is NOT!" I yelled back, but I was already heading for the back door. Sometimes you have to let kids make their own mistakes, and sometimes you have to step in and rescue your overly-enthusiastic child from a rabid chicken. Or vice versa.

The overgrown backyard was a scene of chaos. Hillary, covered in what I hoped was just mud, was chasing a surprisingly agile chicken in circles while several more pecked casually at what had once been a vegetable garden. I made a mental note to add "buy chicken-proof fencing" to my ever-growing list, right after "unpack office" and "figure out what's living in the attic."

"Hillary Ann Kovak, stop chasing that chicken!" I used my Mom Voice, the one that worked on everyone except my own actual children.

"But this is the chicken that stole my sandwich!" She paused her pursuit long enough to gesture dramatically at the chicken, which took the opportunity to dart between her legs.

"It was in the house?" I gasped.

"No, it was in the treehouse," she clarified.

"I'm not sure that thing is safe, baby. I asked you to stay out of it until I have a chance to check it out." Add it to the list, I thought, and pinched the bridge of my nose. "And we have a perfectly good table in the kitchen."

"Yeah, but Frances was in there," she replied, as if this explained everything. Actually, it kind of did. "Her teenage angst makes everything taste bad."

From inside, I heard Frances yell, "I heard that, you little freak!"

The reddish brown chicken that had started this whole mess strutted past me like it owned the place. I swear it gave me a smirk as it went by.

"See?" Hillary pointed accusingly. "That one's the ring-leader. It's organizing them against us."

I looked at my youngest daughter, covered in filth, hair wild, eyes bright with the thrill of the chase, and snorted with laughter. "Honey, I don't think chickens are capable of organizing a coup."

"Was that a chicken pun, Mom? Really?" Frances had appeared in the doorway, empty plate in hand and eyebrow raised in judgment.

"I'm not apologizing for who I am," I replied, flopping down onto one of the old wooden Adirondack chairs that peppered the backyard. The sun was starting to set and lights were popping on in the valley below us.

I turned back to Hillary. "Do you have any homework this weekend?"

"Nope," she muttered, kicking at the sparse grass.

"That's nice! How was your first week at the new school?" I ran my hand over the rough wood of the chair. There were traces of a pretty blue paint embedded in the grain, but weather had stripped the surface down to a dull gray.

"It sucked," she said flatly. "But this school is only slightly worse than the last one."

"That's...good. I guess." I turned to Frances, who still stood in the doorway to the kitchen. "How was the high school?"

She frowned at me, but her lips said, "It's fine."

"Really?" I couldn't hide my surprise at what—in context—was roaring approval.

Hillary snorted, rifling through her pockets. "She just likes it because she's already made friends who are just as nerdy as she is."

"Really?" I repeated, my voice edging up in optimism.

"Seriously though, whose chickens are these?" Frances asked in an obvious effort to change the subject.

"Oh, they're the neighbor's," Hillary said, now trying to tempt one closer with what looked like half a Pop-Tart she'd produced from thin air. "He told me their names but I don't remember. I think they're in Spanish."

"Mr. Vázquez talked to you?" My interest was piqued. Our closest neighbor had to be in his seventies, but he was out working his little farm down the road every day. We had so far only communicated through waves and random gifts of produce left on our porch.

"Yeah, he's nice! He gave me tomatoes yesterday when I was playing by the fence." Hillary had successfully lured the chicken within grabbing distance. "Can we get chickens of our own, Mom? Please?"

"Absolutely not." I watched as the chicken snatched the Pop-Tart and bolted. Hillary lunged after it and ended up sprawled face-first in the dirt. "We are definitely not equipped for livestock."

"That's what Dad would have said," Frances muttered, turning to go back inside.

I felt that familiar twist in my gut, the one that always came when one of my girls mentioned their father. "Your father would have hired someone to handle it, and then figured out how to write it off as a business expense."

Frances paused in the doorway. For a moment, I thought I saw a hint of a smile, but then it was gone. "Whatever. I'm going to my room to die of boredom. There's leftover pasta in the microwave for you."

I blinked. "You made extra?"

"Don't make it weird, Mom." She disappeared inside, but my heart was a little lighter.

Progress, maybe?

A chicken clucked nearby, reminding me of our current situation. "Okay, Hills, new mission: help me herd these things out of the yard."

"Can we use the water gun?"

"Absolutely not."

"Ugh, fine." She stood up, brushing dirt from her knees. "I'll just use my natural chicken-whispering abilities."

"Your what now?"

She made a series of truly disturbing clucking noises. To my amazement, two of the chickens actually looked up.

"See? I speak their language."

"I'm not sure whether to be impressed or concerned," I admitted, watching as she began herding the birds toward the gate with her chicken calls.

"Both," I muttered to myself. "Definitely both."

2

Saturday Morning

Saturday morning dawned with the kind of perfect fall weather that makes you forget about killer chickens and moody teenagers. Of course, my peaceful morning coffee on the back porch lasted approximately thirty seconds before reality crashed in.

My phone was ringing, the special tone I'd set for work emergencies. Because apparently that was how this day was going to go..

"Jane! Thank god you answered!" My boss's voice was pitched higher than usual. "The CEO's gone completely off the rails."

I snorted. "At eight o'clock on a Saturday morning?"

"He's calling everyone into the office," Jim exclaimed. "Be grateful you're not local anymore."

"I am." I took another sip of my coffee. "So what does he want?"

"He wants all of the branding changed to red. Everything. By Monday."

I rolled my eyes and laughed. "Of course he does."

"Can you help? I know it's the weekend, but—"

"I can do it," I sighed. "But I'm submitting it as overtime."

"Done. You're a lifesaver."

I ended the call just as Hillary's voice carried through three closed doors and possibly into the next county. "Mom! We're out of cereal!"

"The horror," I muttered into my coffee cup. "How will we survive?"

She appeared in the doorway, still in her sassy hippo pajamas. "And bread. Also, Frances used the last of the shampoo."

From upstairs came an indignant, "Did not!"

I took another fortifying sip of coffee. "Sounds like we need to do a grocery run."

Frances appeared at the top of the stairs, her hair wrapped in a towel. "The last time we went to the grocery store in town, Hills tried to ride the cart down the dairy aisle and knocked over an entire display of yogurt."

"That was one time," Hillary protested.

"We're probably banned," her sister shot back.

I stood up, decision made. "Okay, here's the deal. If you both come with me and behave like somewhat civilized humans, we can each get one completely unnecessary item of our choosing."

There was a calculating silence.

"Define unnecessary," Frances said finally.

"Nothing alive, nothing that requires assembly, and nothing that would make the health department nervous."

"Deal!" Hillary bounced on her toes. "I want blue hair dye!"

"Absolutely not," Frances and I said together.

It was a solid forty-five minutes before both girls were dressed and walking out of the house, which I counted as a win. Frances got into the car and Hillary ran to the end of the drive to open our gate as a jacked-up pickup truck flew past. A cloud of brown dust rose in his wake and settled over the rosebushes that lined the fence and my poor kid. I pulled through the gate and waited as Hillary pushed it shut again and hopped into the back seat.

"That guy was smokin'!" she said, coughing a little and waving at the dust that had followed her into the car.

I frowned in the direction the truck had disappeared and started down the mountain. "Yeah," I muttered. "Not sure why he's in such a hurry on a Saturday morning."

I noticed Mr. Vázquez standing outside his house as we got closer. He waved and headed toward us with a basket and I pulled the car to a stop.

"Quick, how do you say 'keep your chickens out of my yard' in Spanish?" I whispered to Frances, who had taken four years of Spanish in school.

"No idea, but I can tell him where the library is and what time the party starts."

Mr. Vázquez approached my window with a smile on his weathered face, offering a basket of what looked like pomegranates.

"Gracias," I managed, accepting the fruit. "Um...sus po llos...muy..." I made vague flying motions with my hands.

He nodded sagely and replied with what sounded like a very long, very rapid explanation in Spanish.

I smiled and nodded, understanding exactly none of it. "Si, si...gracias."

As we drove away, Hillary announced from the back-seat, "That was painful to watch."

"Your face is painful to watch," I replied maturely.

The drive down the mountain was always an adventure in itself. We were stuck behind a ginormous tractor for half a mile, which was taking up the entire road while moving at approximately the speed of continental drift. I waved cheerfully as it finally turned onto one of the fields and we zipped past.

On the right there was a fairly new mobile home with an actual picket fence and a late model SUV in the driveway. Then we passed what the girls had dubbed "the drug house," a surprisingly modern structure that always seemed to have at least a dozen cars parked around it.

"Drug dealers," Frances said knowingly.

"We don't know that."

She rolled her eyes. "Mom, nobody has that many friends over this early on a Saturday."

"Maybe they're having a book club meeting," I suggested weakly.

"Sure, Mom. A book club. With guys who look like extras from *Breaking Bad*."

At the end of our road, we had to stop for the cheerful British lady who lived in the little cottage there. She was walking her goat. On a leash. Because apparently that's just country life.

"Good morning!" she called in her crisp accent. "Lovely day, isn't it?"

The goat bleated in agreement and I gave them both a wave.

The small grocery store at the edge of the town was mercifully quiet, though there were a few clusters of people having intense conversations throughout the shockingly empty aisles. I caught snippets as we shopped.

"...my sister in Richmond heard..."

"...closing schools in three counties..."

"...just like that movie where..."

I directed the girls to the cereal aisle. Pickings were slim, which cut down on the arguments. After they made their selections, I cut them loose.

"Okay, remember the rules: one unnecessary item each, and Hillary–" I gave her a stern look. "No hair dye."

"This is literally the worst store ever," Frances complained, scanning the limited offerings as her sister skipped away. "They don't even have spicy mayo."

"It's not usually this bad," I pointed out. "They have regular mayo," I added helpfully, snagging the last loaf of bread on the shelf.

"Oh my god, Mom, what planet are you from? This is basically child abuse."

"Noted. I'll be sure to mention that to my parole officer."

We managed to get through our list without any major incidents, though Hillary was disappointed to find the store only carried a small selection of completely normal brown and blonde hair dyes. She settled for a giant bag of gummy worms. Frances chose a magazine that cost more than my first car, and I treated myself to a bottle of really nice olive oil.

As we pulled out of the tiny grocery store parking lot, I decided it was time for one of those mother-daughter talks that always seem to go better in movies than in real life.

"So...how are you guys doing? With, you know, everything?" I stole a glance over at Frances in time to see her eyes roll.

"Mom," she groaned, "are we really doing this now?"

"Yes, because you can't escape from a moving vehicle."

"Watch me," Hillary muttered from the back seat.

I pressed on as I turned toward home and the road started climbing. "I know the move has been hard. And the divorce..." I let the sentence trail off into an awkward silence.

"Dad sent me a text yesterday," Frances said abruptly. "He's taking his secretary to Paris."

The steering wheel creaked ominously in my grip. "Of course he is."

"He said he'd take us next time."

"Right after he takes us to Florida?" Hillary piped up as we pulled up to our gate. "Or after he comes to my dance recital? Or maybe after he remembers my birthday isn't in July?"

I drew the car to a stop and turned to look at her in surprise.

"What?" She shrugged, opening her car door. "I'm eight, not stupid." She hopped out of the car and opened the gate.

As soon as I parked the car, I jumped out and pulled Hillary into a hug. "I'm sorry everything's different now. But we're going to be okay. We've got each other, and a house full of weird wallpaper. And chickens, apparently."

"And drug dealer neighbors," Frances added helpfully, disappearing into the house with the groceries.

"Book club," I corrected automatically, following her with the basket of pomegranates. "Now, what do I do with these?"

"Trash?" Frances suggested.

"Are you kidding? We're country folk now. We need to learn to live off the land."

"Worst. Mom. Ever."

3

Saturday Midday

Hector

"Must be a full moon," Ted muttered as they rolled their specially modified Haro PD4 police issue mountain bikes up to the third call of the shift. This one was at a cute little cafe in the pedestrian only area of Old Town, where dispatch reported a customer causing a disturbance.

Hector snorted as he swung his leg over his bike. "Full moon's not for another week, partner. People are just pissed that there might be another mask mandate next week." He unbuckled his helmet and adjusted his regulation mask over the bottom half of his face. The fabric matched his uniform and fit snugly over the bridge of his nose.

"I'm grateful for the masks," Ted shot him a smirk. "Means I don't have to watch women moon over your chiseled good looks."

"Shut up." Hector rolled his eyes as they walked to the cafe entrance.

"The shorts are bad enough, man," Ted snickered, opening the door.

The scene that greeted them inside was pure chaos. A middle-aged woman in expensive athleisure wear was throwing pastries at baristas while screaming about her coffee order.

"Richmond Police, Ma'am," Hector called out in his most reasonable voice. "Let's step outside and talk about what's bothering you."

The woman whirled around, and Hector felt his stomach drop. Her eyes were bloodshot, and her pale face glistened with sweat.

"I ordered a VENTI!" she shrieked, hurling a blueberry scone with surprising accuracy. "A Venti! A Venti!" She looked down at the empty display of pastries and whipped her head toward us. "Everything is wrong!" she screamed.

Ted stepped forward, hands raised placatingly. "Ma'am, we can sort this out, but you need to calm—"

She lunged at Ted with shocking speed, teeth bared. "I'll kill you!"

"What the actual fuck," Hector muttered, grabbing her arms while Ted restrained her legs. She was unnaturally strong, thrashing and snapping like a rabid animal.

"This is definitely above my pay grade," Ted grunted as they struggled to get her on the ground. "We're gonna need a bus."

When the EMTs arrived, it took all four of them to hold her down for sedation. As they loaded her into the ambulance, one of the paramedics shook his head.

"Fifth one like this today," he said. "She's definitely going to be positive for this new virus. People are losing their damn minds."

Before Hector could respond, the radio clipped to his shoulder crackled. "Unit 247, we have a 10-31 at 723 Old Town Square. Subject is violent and destructive."

Ted sighed. "No rest for the wicked. Let's go deal with another entitled asshole having a bad day."

"Copy that," Hector responded into his radio, already moving. "Unit 247 responding."

The ride through the Old Town weekend traffic was short. Ted checked his phone as they left the bikes and entered the lobby of the commercial office space.

"Still no vote on the mask requirements," he reported. "They're reporting fewer than a thousand cases in the state."

Hector glanced over in disbelief as he held open the door for his partner. "We've got ten times that just in the city," he scoffed.

"Yeah, but they don't count until they get the test results back, and that's taking days." Ted shrugged. "Just keep your mask on and your hands clean and we'll get through this."

The security guard at the desk in the lobby waved them through, a look of relief on his face. The elevator doors opened as they approached, spilling out several harassed millennials in business casual wear.

"Busy for a Saturday afternoon," Ted noted as they stepped into the car and it began to rise.

The elevator doors opened onto an open plan workspace. Employees huddled together in cubicles, whispering and pointing toward the corner office. A man in an expensive suit rushed to meet them.

"Thank god you're here," he said, mopping his brow with a handkerchief. "He's been in there for hours, screaming about everything being the wrong color."

Ted pulled out his notebook. "And you are?"

"I'm Jim Wilson, the VP of Marketing. Brad Schmidt is our CEO. He called everyone into the office this morning and kept asking for changes. But none of what he was asking for was making sense. He just got angrier and angrier and then he started throwing stuff every time someone tried to enter his office. I think he might be on something."

Hector approached the office cautiously. Through the glass wall, he could see a man pacing back and forth, talking to himself and rubbing at his eyes.

Wilson took a deep breath and lowered his voice. "He picked up the chair by his desk and threw it at the window." His gaze moved to the office, brow furrowed in concern, before turning back to meet Hector's eyes. "That's when I called 911."

"You did the right thing," Hector told him, patting him on the shoulder. "Why don't you go ahead and send everyone home?"

Hector watched the VP scamper back down the hallway toward the cubicles before knocking lightly on the CEO's office.

Ted approached the office door. "Mr. Schmidt? I'm Officer Lemon. Why don't you come talk to us about what's bothering you?"

Schmidt's head snapped up, pinning Ted with bloodshot eyes. "Red...it should all be RED!" he screamed, grabbing a letter opener from his desk.

"Ted, get back!" Hector shouted, but it was too late.

Schmidt moved with inhuman speed, driving the letter opener into Ted's shoulder.

The gunshot was deafening in the enclosed space.

Schmidt dropped, a neat hole in his chest. His body thrashed on the patterned carpet, like an up-ended turtle. He kept trying to get up, muttering about red.

"Shit," Ted sighed, letting his gun fall to his side and clutching his bleeding shoulder with the other hand. "This is going to be a lot of paperwork."

***

The ER was packed with people exhibiting the same symptoms as Schmidt and the Karen: red eyes, disorientation, and aggression. A lot of aggression. Medical staff in protective gear rushed between patients restrained to their beds.

"Officer?" A doctor wearing a full mask with a plastic shield pulled Hector aside. "They're taking your partner up to surgery. He should be fine but there's nothing more you can do for now."

"Thanks, doctor." Hector searched the man's tired face. "How is Schmidt, the guy with the gunshot wound?"

The doctor shook his head. "He didn't make it. I'm sorry."

"I know you did your best." Hector fiddled with the loop of his standard issue cloth mask where it rubbed at the top of his ear. "My partner shot him." He glanced around the barely contained chaos of the ER. "Did he have this virus thing?"

"It's not a virus," the doctor corrected automatically. "But yes, he was almost definitely at an advanced stage of a GRM or GRMp infection, which should clear your partner in the shooting." The doctor's eyes were haunted.

"Once the infection progresses, patients have to be re-strained." He shuddered. "You should get out of here."

As if to emphasize his point, screams erupted from a nearby treatment room, followed by the sound of breaking equipment and shouting.

4

Saturday Afternoon

I was elbow-deep in pomegranate guts, a YouTube tu-torial playing on my phone, when Frances cleared her throat behind me. The sound was tentative in a way that immediately put me on high alert.

"So," she began, examining her nails with forced casual-ness, "I may have made a few friends at school."

I carefully kept my face neutral, though my heart did a little happy dance. "Oh?"

"Yeah, just a couple of girls from my grade. They're kind of cool, I guess." She shrugged, still not meeting my eyes. "They wanted to maybe hang out this weekend and do homework."

"That would be great!" I winced internally at how eager I sounded. "I mean, that's cool. Whatever."

She rolled her eyes, but I caught the hint of a smile. "So, like, maybe they could come over?"

"Of course! When were you thinking?"

The doorbell rang.

Frances's face went through several expressions in rapid succession, landing somewhere between guilty and defiant. "Um, now?"

"Frances Elizabeth Kovak!"

"You said it was fine!"

"I meant theoretically fine, not immediately fine!" I looked down at my juice-stained hands in horror. "I'm sticky!"

She was already heading for the door. "No one expects you to shake hands. Just be normal."

"Am I ever?" I called after her, frantically washing my hands.

I heard the door open and multiple teenage voices filled the entryway. By the time I'd dried my hands and emerged from the kitchen, Frances had already whisked her friends upstairs. I caught a glimpse of two girls, both looking far more put together than I currently did in my ancient college sweatshirt and paint-splattered yoga pants.

"Nice to meet you!" I called up the stairs.

"Mom!" Frances's mortified voice drifted down. "Stop!"

"Love you too, honey!"

The sound of a door slamming was my only response. I returned to my pomegranate massacre sporting a huge grin. The fact that Frances felt comfortable enough to bring friends over, even if she was embarrassed by my existence, was a major win.

The doorbell rang again.

"If that's another random teenager, I'm instituting a strict RSVP policy!" I called out, wiping my hands again.

But when I opened the door, it was an older man wearing jeans and a button down shirt. He gave me an overly white, toothy smile that immediately set my teeth on edge.

"Mrs. Kovak," he drawled smarmily.

His hand was on the storm door and he gave it a tug but it held firm. I sent a silent thanks to Frances for remembering to lock it. The storm door had a tendency to fly open with the slightest breeze, so I'd been reminding the girls to lock it every time we came in.

I gave Mr. Smarmy a polite smile through the screen. "That's right. How can I help you?"

"Just wanted to stop by to introduce myself and have a friendly chat about property lines." He pulled out a folded paper from his pocket. "I'm Clyde Johnson and I own most of the land up here, including the orchard at the top of the mountain."

"That's nice," I said flatly.

He unfolded what appeared to be a survey map. "That retaining wall on your south side? It's over my property line by about six inches."

I blinked. "The wall that's been there for like fifty years?"

"Bob Peterson and I had a gentleman's agreement but he never got around to fixing it before he sold." He smiled, showing too many teeth. "Course, I hear you got quite a settlement in your divorce. Took your husband to the cleaners, is the talk in town."

Fighting the urge to slam the door in his face, I let my smile fall away. "My personal finances are none of your concern, Mr. Johnson."

"No offense meant, little lady. I've got nothing but respect for a woman who knows her own worth." His smile widened. "I'd be happy to discuss the matter over dinner."

My frown deepened.

After an awkward pause, Johnson's smile slipped and he continued. "I'm just saying, I'd be willing to sell you that strip of land. Save us both the hassle of a lawsuit." He named a figure that was near to what I'd paid for the entire property and I held back a snort. "Think about it. Not for long, though. My lawyer's pretty eager to file those papers."

"Thank you for bringing this to my attention. I'll have my lawyer look into it." I closed the door in his face. Maybe not technically a slam, but definitely with more force than strictly necessary.

"What a spectacular jackass," I muttered, heading back to the kitchen.

It was time to get some work done, so I shoved the mess I'd made of the pomegranates into the fridge. I was tempted to trash them but the mental image of the judgment on Frances' face if she found out held me back.

Hillary walked into the kitchen and began rifling through the drawers without a word.

"Whatcha looking for, kiddo?" I asked, washing my hands one more time to get rid of the last of the stickiness from the fruit.

"Food coloring," she muttered without looking up, clawing through the junk drawer.

Drying my hands on a tea towel, I nodded toward the next drawer. "One more down."

Hillary opened the second drawer and pounced on a bottle of blue food dye with an, "Aha!" and scrambled back out of the room while my brain was still processing.

Oh, crap.

"Hills!" I shouted. "If any of that dye gets on the bathroom tile, you're regrouting it yourself!"

Priorities.

***

I was just emerging from design hell, when Hillary appeared at my elbow looking like a demented Smurf.

"Mom," she said firmly, "Frances and her nerdy friends are in my treehouse."

I fired off the email I was writing and took a deep breath, struggling up through my post-work fog. "You're very blue, honey."

"I think they're summoning demons."

"Demons?" I questioned, raising one skeptical eyebrow. "I told you both to stay out of the treehouse. That thing is a death trap."

I headed for the back door and Hillary trailed me across the backyard. The ancient treehouse loomed above us, fairy lights twinkling in the gathering dusk.

Wait. Fairy lights?

"How did they get electricity up there?"

Hillary shrugged. "Extension cord from the garage. They have candles, too."

"That's probably a fire hazard." Although kind of impressive, I admitted to myself. "Frances Elizabeth Kovak!"

There was a scrambling sound from above, followed by teenage shushing noises.

"If you're planning to burn down the treehouse, at least let me check our insurance coverage first!" Was a treehouse considered an ancillary structure?

Frances's head appeared in the window. "Mom! You're embarrassing me!"

"Yes, that's my job, dear. You'd better not have an open flame up there."

Frances came down the ladder with her binder in one hand, looking murderous. The two other girls following behind her more slowly, each weighed down with backpacks.

"It's out. We were just doing homework," Frances muttered.

"With fairy lights and candles?"

"For ambiance," one of her friends offered helpfully. She was short and round like a kewpie doll, with a riot of light brown curls falling down to the center of her back. "I'm Ivy, by the way. And that's Taylor."

The other girl, a tall blonde, waved. "Nice to meet you, Mrs. Kovak." She nudged my daughter and stage-whispered, "Your mom's cool, Frances."

Frances looked like she might spontaneously combust. "She's really not."

"I like her," I agreed cheerfully, reaching down to unplug the extension cord from the treehouse lights. "Would you guys like some pizza? You can eat while I tell you embarrassing stories about Frances as a baby."

"Mom!"

"I'm just kidding!" I told her as I herded everyone back into the house. "I have pictures," I whispered loudly to Taylor.

The next hour was surprisingly pleasant. I heated up a couple of frozen pizzas and the girls chatted while we demolished them, and I learned more about my daughter's social life than I had in months. Both girls were in all of Frances' advanced classes. Taylor was a theater kid and trying to talk Frances and Ivy into trying out for the school's production of *Annie*. Both girls played field hockey and Ivy, despite her lack of height, was also on the basketball team. The girls made plans to watch her next game.

"Will your parents be there?" I asked.

Ivy shook her head. "It's just me and my mom and she works a lot," the girl said matter-of-factly.

"Can I go, Mom?" Frances asked. When I hesitated, she narrowed her eyes. "Of course, if I had my driver's license—"

"I'll take you," I rushed in, not ready to have this argument again.

"Can I go, too?" Hillary joined in, looking up from the elaborate structure she was making out of pomegranate seeds.

I nodded, both alarmed and relieved to see that the blue dye covering my child was wiping off onto everything she touched.

Later, Frances walked her friends outside when Ivy's mom arrived to take them back to town and I sent Hillary upstairs to give herself a good scrub. I had finished clearing the table when she came back into the dining room much less blue, but with a concerned look on her face.

"Mom," she said suddenly, "the lady on the news seems really worried."

It was just after five, so the news shouldn't be running yet. I followed Hillary into the living room and, sure enough, an anchor sitting behind a desk dominated the screen with a serious expression. The image abruptly transitioned to a reporter standing outside what appeared to be a hospital in the city.

"...authorities are advising people to stay home if possible. The CDC has confirmed that the rate of GRM prion infections..."

I switched it off as Frances walked back into the house. "Just another virus. Hopefully you guys won't have to wear masks to school again." I shook my head and smiled. "Remember when your father bought all of those boxes of masks made out of mesh."

Frances snorted. "Yeah, and then he tried to sell them online as 'upgraded'."

"Designer editions," I corrected, and we both laughed and shared a smile.

Yup, my ex-husband was a tool.

Frances's expression turned serious. "Thanks," she said quietly. "For not being completely horrible."

I clutched my chest dramatically. "Be still my beating heart! Was that actual gratitude from my teenage daughter?"

She rolled her eyes, but there was definitely a hint of a smile in there. "Whatever. I'm going to bed."

"Love you too, honey."

5

Sunday Morning

Sunday dawned crisp and clear on the mountain, the kind of perfect fall morning that makes you question every life choice that led you to living in a city in the first place. I stood at the kitchen sink, coffee in hand, as the sun crept over the valley below us. The town was still shrouded in mist, making the scattered houses look like islands in a cotton candy sea.

"Stop staring out the window and make breakfast," Frances grumbled, shuffling past me in her fuzzy unicorn slippers. "Some of us are starving."

"Good morning to you too, sunshine," I called after her. "Love the bedhead!"

She flipped me off without turning around, which I chose to interpret as a sign of affection.

We were all up and moving by the time the haze burned off. In a spurt of uncharacteristic domestic energy, I grabbed a broom and began sweeping the fallen leaves from our wide front porch. The view really was spectacular here. From this side of the house I could see all the way down to the drug house—sorry, book club. It was quiet for once, though there were still an impressive number of vehicles parked at the front of the property.

A movement caught my eye and I spotted a couple walking an enormous dog along the road. They waved and changed course, heading toward our gate.

"Hills!" I called through the screen door. "Put on pants! We have company!"

"You're not my real mom!" she shouted, thundering up the stairs.

"You wish!" I called after her.

By the time I made it to the fence, Hillary emerged from the house behind me, mostly presentable.

"Morning!" the woman called out cheerfully as I opened the gate. Her husband nodded hello while struggling to control their dog, who was as determined to greet Hillary as she was to be greeted.

"Hi," Hillary said, running up beside me and throwing herself to the ground so the dog could give her a thorough face licking.

"I'm so sorry," the mom gushed. "Sit, Zeus! Sit."

The dog completely ignored her.

"That's okay," Hillary told her, rubbing the big block head behind its ears. "I speak dog."

The woman laughed in relief. "I'm Sarah and this is Tom." She looked at him expectantly but he just frowned at her. She shrugged and turned back to me with a wide smile. "We're number twelve. We just wanted to stop by and introduce ourselves properly. We've seen you all settling in but haven't had a chance to say hello."

"That's so kind," I said, meaning it. "Would you like some coffee? Fair warning though, my eldest daughter made it and it might strip paint."

"I heard that!" Frances called faintly from the house.

"You were meant to!" I yelled over my shoulder.

Sarah's eyes crinkled with amusement. "We can't stay, but I wanted to say hi. It's not often we get new neighbors up here. We're staying in the trailer at the moment, but we're about to break ground on a new house."

"Thank you for coming by," I replied. "Definitely feel free to stop by anytime. Obviously, we love dogs." I waved at the lovefest happening at Sarah's feet. "Though I should warn you, Hillary's going through a blue period." There were blue smudges still visible on my daughter's exposed skin.

"Mom!" Hillary's protest was muffled by the fact that her face was buried in the dog's scruff. "I'm expressing myself!"

"Like a Smurf," I added helpfully.

Tom spoke up for the first time. "Watch out for the guy at the top of the road, Clyde. There's something wrong with him." Tom turned to glare up the mountain.

Sarah laughed. "It's true. He's been trying to sell that strip of land along your property line for years. He used to harass poor Bob, the previous owner, on a weekly basis."

"Already had that pleasure," I grimaced. "Is he always so..."

"Aggressively creepy?" Sarah supplied. "Yes. Yes, he is. He tried to sue us over our mailbox. He claimed it was too close to the road."

"Did he win?"

"Nope," she grinned. "And he was pissed."

We chatted for a few more minutes before they headed back down the mountain, Tom dragging Zeus away from Hillary.

"They seem nice," I told Frances when Hillary and I walked back into the house.

"Yeah," Hillary agreed. "Too bad they're probably serial killers."

I turned to stare at her. "What?"

She shrugged. "Nobody's that friendly without ulterior motives."

"You're too young to be that cynical, Hills."

"I get it from my mother."

The rest of the morning passed in a blur of home improvement projects. We managed to unpack the last boxes in my office and started stripping the wallpaper, revealing some truly impressive water damage that I was definitely going to ignore for now. The girls actually worked together to organize the garage without being bribed.

After lunch, we tackled the garden. The previous owner had let it go wild, but there were good bones under all the weeds. We worked steadily through the afternoon, sorting what might be salvageable from what definitely needed to go.

"Mom," Hillary called from behind a massive hydrangea bush. "I found another chicken!"

"Is it alive?" I asked warily.

"Nope!"

"Then leave it alone and go wash your hands!"

Frances emerged from the shed covered in cobwebs. "I found the previous owner's collection of garden gnomes. They're...disturbing."

"Define disturbing."

She held up what appeared to be a rather well-endowed ceramic gnome. "I'm pretty sure this one is cursed."

"Perfect," I said brightly. "We'll put it right by the front door to ward off Clyde."

Speaking of the devil, a familiar pickup truck rumbled past our gate, slowing just enough for its driver to glare at us. I waved cheerfully, which seemed to annoy him even more.

"Mom," Frances said seriously. "You're going to get us murdered."

"Probably," I agreed. "But at least we'll die with our property lines intact."

The sun was setting by the time we called it quits, painting the sky in shades of orange and pink that made me forget about cursed gnomes and creepy neighbors. We sat on the back porch, drinking lemonade and watching the light fade from the valley below.

"This doesn't completely suck," Frances admitted quietly.

"High praise indeed." I bumped her shoulder with mine. "Now help me figure out what to do with all those pomegranates before they go bad."

"Throw them at that big truck every time it drives past our house?"

"Frances!"

"What? It was just a suggestion."

6

Monday Morning

My phone buzzed and I slapped at the nightstand blindly until I found it, bringing it close to my face before opening my eyes. The light streaming through my windows was far too bright.

"Oh no," I muttered, squinting at my phone. "No, no, no..."

The words "Emergency All Hands Meeting 10AM" floated in a bubble at the bottom of the screen, but what caught my attention was the 8:47 AM that glared at me accusingly from the top of the screen.

"GIRLS!" I screeched, launching myself out of bed. "UP! NOW!"

Silence.

I pulled on pants and stumbled down the hall, barging into Frances's room without knocking. The lump under her comforter didn't stir.

"Frances! We overslept!"

She emerged like a grumpy butterfly from her cocoon of blankets. "So?"

"You're going to be late for school." I checked my phone again. "It's Monday!"

She blinked at me owlishly.

"Why didn't you wake me up?" I asked plaintively, throwing my hands in the air.

"I'm not your alarm clock," she mumbled, rolling over and burrowing back under her covers.

I closed my eyes and counted to ten. When I opened them, Frances was snoring softly.

Hillary's room was empty, but I found her in the kitchen eating cereal and watching cartoons on her tablet.

"Morning, Mom!" She waved her spoon cheerfully. "I made coffee!"

I looked at the coffee maker. It was, indeed, on, though what was in it looked more like tar than coffee.

"Hills, honey, why didn't you wake me up?"

She shrugged. "You looked like you needed the rest."

"You're going to be late," I pointed out, pouring myself a cup of black sludge that I hoped wouldn't kill me. "Please go get dressed."

"Can't we just stay home?" She gave me her best puppy dog eyes. "It's already so late..."

"Nice try, but no. Education is important." I took a sip of the coffee and immediately dumped the mug into the sink and regretted all of my life choices. "Go wake up your sister and put some clothes on."

"But Mom..."

"Now, please."

She slouched off, muttering dark threats under her breath. Dear god, I hoped that Frances grew out of her moody phase before Hillary entered hers, or none of us would make it.

I ran upstairs and brushed my teeth for about fifteen seconds and threw on a bra. There were sounds of life coming from the girls' rooms, so I threw on my shoes and ran outside to start the car. Hunching my shoulders against the brisk fall mountain air, I slid into the driver's seat of my very practical, very reliable mom-mobile.

I jammed the key into the ignition and turned it.

Nothing happened.

I tried again.

Still nothing.

"You have got to be kidding me." I dropped my head onto the steering wheel, which caused the horn to blast and almost made me pee myself.

"Everything okay out there?" Frances called from the doorway, still in her pajamas.

"Just peachy," I replied through gritted teeth. "The car won't start."

"Oh no," she deadpanned. "Whatever shall we do?"

I glared at her. "Your sarcasm is not helping."

"My sarcasm is delightful." She yawned and stretched. "So, does this mean we can stay home?"

I checked the time. It was after nine. My all-hands meeting was in less than an hour. Frances wasn't dressed. Hillary was still upstairs. Even if I could get the car started, I'd never make it down the mountain and back in time.

"Fine," I sighed. "But this is a one-time thing. And you both have to actually do your schoolwork."

"Yes!" Hillary appeared behind her sister, somehow already changed and ready for the day. "Can we have pancakes?"

"No, because I have a meeting in forty-five minutes and I need to take a shower so that I look like a functional human being." I gestured at my current state of dishevelment.

Frances snorted. "Good luck with that. Your hair looks like you stuck your finger in an electrical socket."

"Thank you for that assessment." I abandoned my dead car and headed for the house. "Try not to burn the place down."

"No promises!" Hillary called after me.

Thirty minutes later, I was somewhat presentable and settled at my desk with a fresh cup of actual coffee. Frances was lying on her bed with a book and Hillary was sprawled out in the middle of the living room, allegedly doing schoolwork.

My computer chimed with the meeting reminder. I clicked the link, mentally preparing myself for another thrilling corporate gathering where we'd all pretend to care about quarterly projections and synergy or whatever.

Faces began popping up in their little boxes, but a lot fewer than I expected. Oh, crap. Had the layoffs already started? The normal pre-meeting chatter was subdued, and when my boss Jim came on screen he looked like death warmed over.

"Good morning, everyone," Jim began briskly, despite his pale face. "I'm afraid I have some difficult news to share."

Oh god, I thought, here it comes. We're all getting fired. I've moved myself to the middle of nowhere assuming I could continue to do this job remotely and now I'm going to have to job hunt from the top of this stupid mountain.

"As some of you may have heard, our CEO Brad Schmidt passed away over the weekend."

Wait, what?

The chat exploded with shocked messages and questions. I vaguely registered people asking about what happened, but my mind was stuck on the fact that I'd just redesigned this man's entire website in cherry red on Saturday.

"While this was obviously a terrible shock," Jim continued with a frown, "I want to assure everyone that the company will continue operating normally. We have contingency plans in place for situations like this."

Someone unmuted themselves to ask, "What happened to Brad?"

The COO's face tightened and he rubbed at his eyes. "There was an incident here in the office on Saturday and Brad was injured. He was transported via ambulance to County General where he succumbed to his injuries."

Well, that wasn't ominous at all. Why did Jim seem so angry?

"For now, we'll be continuing with business as usual. Brad would have wanted that."

Would he, though? I wondered. The man once had a meltdown because someone handed out the wrong kind of sparkling water at a board meeting.

The rest of the call passed in a blur of corporate platitudes and vague assurances about job security. By the time it ended, my coffee was cold and my anxiety was through the roof.

"Everything okay in there?" Frances appeared in my doorway. "You look like you've seen a ghost."

"The head of the company died," I said flatly.

She blinked. "The sparkling water guy?"

"That's the one."

"Karma's a bitch."

"Frances!"

"What? He sounded like an ass." She perched on the edge of my desk. "Are you worried about your job?"

Sometimes I forgot how perceptive she could be.

"A little," I admitted. "New management usually means changes. And changes mean layoffs."

"We'll be fine," she said firmly. "The house is paid for and we've got savings, right? And if worse comes to worst, we can always eat Hillary."

"I heard that!" Hillary shouted from the living room.

"You were meant to!"

I laughed despite myself. "Thank you, both of you. Now please tell me you've done some actual schoolwork?"

"Define actual," Frances hedged.

"That's what I thought." I shut my laptop and stood up. "Okay, new plan. We're going to check the car battery, and then maybe we can make those pancakes."

"Can we put blue food coloring in them?" Hillary yelled.

"Absolutely not."

The pancakes were blue, of course, despite my explicit instructions. Hillary had managed to sneak food coloring into the batter while I was distracted trying to YouTube my way through basic car maintenance. The result was a stack of perfectly fluffy pancakes that looked like they'd been cooked by a Smurf.

"They taste the same," Hillary insisted, drowning hers in syrup.

"They look radioactive," Frances commented, but she was already on her second serving.

I had to admit, they were pretty good. Even if I suspected I was failing some fundamental test of responsible adulting. At least the coffee was drinkable.

"So what's the verdict on the car?" Frances asked around a mouthful of blue breakfast.

"Well," I began, trying to sound confident, "according to seventeen different YouTube mechanics, it's probably the battery. Or the starter. Or the alternator. Or the flux capacitor." I covered my eyes with my hands. "Or ghosts."

"Ghosts?" Hillary perked up. "Can we get a priest to perform an exorcism?"

"No."

"What about—"

"I called the mechanic in town but they can't come up until Wednesday." I pushed my plate away and pulled my laptop closer, ignoring my child.

Frances raised an eyebrow. "And how exactly are we getting to town for groceries and stuff if the car doesn't start?"

"We just got groceries. And I'm working on it." I wasn't, actually.

I was desperately trying not to spiral into a panic about money. The move had cleaned out a good chunk of my savings. The divorce settlement and my half of the equity in our brownstone had covered the cost of this place, thank god, but there were still property taxes and utilities and two growing kids who needed things like food and clothes and apparently regular doses of food coloring.

And now my very steady, very reliable remote job might be in jeopardy because my CEO had randomly dropped dead. Perfect. If I lost my health insurance—

A knock at the door saved me from descending further into financial anxiety. Hillary bounded up to answer it.

"It's Mr. Vázquez!" she called out cheerfully. "The chicken man!"

"Hillary!" I hissed, mortified, standing behind her. "Don't call him that!"

But our elderly neighbor just smiled and held out a small metal object. A padlock and key?

"Gracias," I said automatically, opening the storm door to accept it. "Um..."

He launched into rapid Spanish, gesturing animatedly. I caught maybe one word in ten, something about "puerta" which I was pretty sure meant door.

Hillary, who had apparently been paying more attention in Spanish class than her sister, piped up. "I think he's talking about our gate?"

Mr. Vázquez nodded enthusiastically and made a locking motion with his hands, then pointed down the mountain. He continued speaking and I caught the last couple of words.

"Close the gate?" I hazarded.

More nodding. He pointed at the key, then at our gate, then at me, then made the locking motion again.

"I think he wants us to keep our gate locked," Hillary translated helpfully.

I had questions, but Mr. Vázquez was already heading back down our driveway, waving goodbye as he went.

"Well, that was weird," Frances commented from behind me.

I closed the door and shrugged, shaking off the feeling of unease. "Maybe he's worried about thieves?"

"What are they going to steal? Our collection of cursed garden gnomes?"

"Hey, those gnomes are valuable family heirlooms."

7
Monday Afternoon

Taylor

Something was wrong. It had been such a weird day at school, and now her father's briefcase was on the floor, papers scattered across the carpet like confetti.

"Dad?" Taylor called out, dropping her backpack by the stairs. "Mom?"

A crash from the kitchen made her jump. Her mother's voice drifted out, shrill and angry. "Everything's wrong! You moved it!"

"I didn't touch anything!" Her father's response was more of a growl than words.

Taylor froze. Her parents never fought. Like, ever. They were the embarrassingly in-love couple that made everyone else uncomfortable with their constant PDAs and inside jokes.

"Mom?" she tried again, edging toward the kitchen. "Are you okay?"

Her mother whirled around and Taylor took an involuntary step back. Her face was chalk-white except for two fever-bright spots high on her cheeks. Her usually perfectly styled hair was a mess, like she'd been running her hands through it repeatedly.

"I need coffee!" Her mother squinted at her, deep furrows marring her usually smooth forehead. "Did you move the coffee? Everything's in the wrong place!"

"I didn't—" Taylor began, but her father cut her off.

"Go to your room," he snapped at her, as if she were twelve. When she hesitated, he slammed his hand down on the counter. "Now!"

Taylor fled up the stairs, her heart pounding. She'd never heard that tone from her father before. He was the guy who got choked up at insurance commercials and insisted on family game night every Sunday.

In her room, she locked the door and curled up on her bed.

The sounds of arguing continued through the afternoon and into the evening, punctuated by more crashes. She looked at her phone and wondered if she should call someone. A lot of people had been missing from school today, including Frances and Ivy. Taylor checked her status, but neither of them were online.

Sitting in the dark, she scrolled through the updates on her feed, seeing video after video of people going crazy in public places and being tazed by the cops. An older woman with short gray hair picked up a chair in a restaurant and threw it at a waitress's head. A guy not much older than Taylor, maybe college age, stood in the middle of the street and banged against the hood of a car until it caved in, speckled with blood from his mangled hands. In one video, a woman jumped onto a police officer's back and bit off his ear.

"Holy crap."

Something heavy hit her bedroom door and Taylor jumped, stifling a yelp.

"Where is the coffee?" Her mother's voice was barely recognizable. "Open this door!"

Another crash against the door made Taylor fly off her bed and crouch down in the space between the bed and the window. Wood splintered around the lock to her door.

"Your mother said open this door!" Her father's voice was a roar.

Taylor scrambled up and began pushing her dresser, maneuvering it in front of her door as quietly as she could. Grabbing her soccer bag from the closet, she dumped out the gear and started shoving random items inside. Phone charger, deodorant, her emergency tampon stash. What else? What did you pack when your parents became homicidal maniacs?

The family photo from her nightstand caught her eye. Last summer at the beach, all three of them smiling and sunburned. She wrapped it in a t-shirt and added it to the bag.

She crept to her window and carefully pushed it open, wincing at every small creak. The old oak tree that had helped her sneak out to countless parties stretched its branches invitingly.

The screen popped out and Taylor tossed her bag down to the ground to land on top of it. The familiar route down the tree was tricky in the darkness, but muscle memory guided her hands and feet.

She was halfway down when light flooded her bedroom. A moment later, her mother's face appeared in the window, cast in shades of red and white like something from a horror movie.

"Go, go, go," Taylor chanted under her breath, scrambling down faster. A branch caught her shirt, tearing it as she yanked free.

Her mother's scream of rage followed her as she hit the ground running. She snatched up her bag without breaking stride and sprinted for the street.

8

Tuesday Morning

My bedroom was too bright. Again. It was also too quiet. No hum of electricity, no chirping phone notifications, no...alarm clock.

I cursed under my breath, fumbling for my phone. Dead. Of course it was dead. I jabbed the power button on my bedside lamp. Nothing.

"Girls!" I yelled, throwing off my covers. "Wake up! We're late! Again."

My feet hit the floor and I yelped at the cold, pulling on my thickest socks.

A muffled "What time is it?" came from Frances's room.

I shoved my legs into an old pair of jeans and threw open her door. Her curtains were closed and it was dark, so I stumbled my way through the random clothes on her floor to make it to the window.

"I don't know what time it is because the power is out and my phone didn't charge," I told her in a rush, letting sunlight flood the room.

When I turned, Frances was sitting up in bed, squinting at her own phone. "I've got two percent," she said. "It's after nine."

"Crap! I missed my morning standup." I ran my hand through my hair, which snagged on several knots. "I'm so getting fired."

"Seriously?" Frances asked, looking more awake.

"No, not seriously," I assured her. "Probably." I crossed to the bed. "Can I borrow your phone to call my boss and let him know what's happening?"

"Sure." Frances unlocked her screen and handed me the phone.

I stood there looking at it blankly.

"What's wrong?" she asked.

"I don't know Jim's number," I admitted. "I don't know anyone's number." I sank onto the edge of the bed. "The only number I can actually remember is my grandmother's house phone from 1987."

I gave Frances her phone back.

"So...um." I took a deep breath and waited for my brain to kick in. "I'm going to go work on the car. Can you get dressed and get Hillary up?"

"Okay." Frances threw off her blankets as I stood up and left her room in a daze.

I started toward the top of the stairs but detoured back into my bedroom and found myself in my bathroom, standing at the sink.

Without a thought in my head, I brushed my teeth and washed my face. I brushed my hair. Then I stood looking at myself in the mirror for way too long.

"Come on, Jane," I said to my reflection. "You've got this."

The middle-aged woman in the mirror didn't look convinced, but it was enough to get me moving again.

When I emerged back into the hallway, Frances was dressed and standing in the doorway to Hillary's room.

"Hillary isn't in her room," she said, frowning.

"Did you check under the bed?" I asked. I wasn't kidding. We'd once been on the verge of calling the police when we'd found her sleeping under her bed. Thank god she snored.

"She's not there," Frances confirmed. "I checked the closet, too."

"I don't have time for a manhunt this morning," I muttered, before taking a deep breath and screaming her name at the top of my lungs. "Hillary!"

"Downstairs!" came the response from below.

Frances was holding her hands over her ears and I grimaced.

"Sorry," I said. "My nerves are shot."

"Well, now mine are too," she snarked. "When was the last time you had coffee?"

I opened my mouth to answer, then closed it again.

"That's what I thought." She headed for the stairs. "I'll make some with the camp stove."

I stared after her blankly. "We have a camp stove?"

"Yeah, it was in the garage behind the box labeled 'Previous Owner's Questionable Life Choices.'"

I followed her downstairs like a puppy and we found Hillary sitting cross-legged on top of the kitchen table eating a pint of ice cream.

"Fridge is dead," she announced, waving her spoon at the offending appliance.

"The power is out," I told her. "Why didn't you wake me up?"

Hillary raised her eyebrows and stared at me over a heaping spoonful of Chunky Monkey. "Why would I do that?"

"You're going to be late for school," I told her in exasperation. "And don't open the fridge. We need the stuff to stay cold until the power comes back on."

Frances emerged from one of the cabinets with a jar of instant coffee.

"You're amazing," I told her sincerely.

"I know." She started to fill the kettle from the tap but the water slowed to a dribble. "Mom..." She swung the handle to the other side and the water started again.

I jumped to my feet. "Stop." I closed the tap and stood there staring at the faucet for a moment, my brain spinning.

"What?" Frances was still standing holding the kettle, staring at me in confusion.

"The pump on the well is electric," I explained. "If the power is out then the water in the hot water heater is all we have in the house until it comes back on." I ran my hands through my hair. "I can't even get any updates from the power company because my phone is dead!"

Frances set the kettle back on the counter and crossed to sit at the table, pulling her phone from her pocket. "I'll check on my phone. You need to breathe."

"*You* need to breathe," I snarked back, then immediately felt guilty. "Sorry! I just need electricity! And I need to get you guys to school!"

Hillary looked up from her ice cream. "I'm pretty sure school is canceled."

"I can't check because we don't have internet!" I waved my arms wildly. "I'm supposed to be working! I have deadlines!"

"Mom—"

"Don't 'Mom' me! This is a disaster! We're going to end up living in a van down by the river!"

"Is that a reference to something?" Hillary stage-whispered to her sister.

"I think she's finally cracked," Frances whispered back.

"I can hear you both!" I ran my hands through my hair, sinking into a chair. "Okay. We need a plan. Frances, can you check the school website, too?"

Frances frowned down at her phone. "I don't have a signal. I'm going to try from outside." She scooted back her chair and headed out of the room.

"Hillary, I'm going to find the emergency radio. Why don't you...I don't know, sacrifice something to the electricity gods."

"How about one of the chickens?" Hillary asked hopefully, standing to dump her empty ice cream carton into the trash.

"Hey, Mom," Frances called. "You should probably come look at this."

"Unless it's the guys from the garage, I don't want to look at anything."

"No, seriously." Frances insisted, sounding strange. "You really need to see this."

I followed her voice through the living room to the back door, Hillary at my heels.

"What are you—" The words died in my throat.

The valley was on fire.

Not just a single building, not just a small blaze. The entire skyline was obscured by thick black smoke, and even from here I could see flames licking at the sky.

"Holy crap," I said quietly.

We stood in silence for a long moment, watching the smoke billow up into the crystal clear morning sky.

"Yeah," Hillary broke the silence, "I'm pretty sure school is canceled."

9

Tuesday Late Morning

Taylor

Taylor woke up in someone's garden shed, a small trowel clutched tightly to her chest. It had taken her hours last night just to make it back to the high school, sticking to the shadows between streetlights. There had been a bunch of car accidents and someone had even hit a house with a big truck.

Everywhere random people were walking the streets—mostly just talking to themselves. Some were running and a few seemed to be fighting with each other. Even after the lights all abruptly died, she'd been able to avoid the violent ones, since they weren't quiet.

When Taylor had made it back to the school, it was locked and empty. Exhausted, she'd ducked into the fenced backyard of a house across the street and shut herself into this garden shed around dawn.

Now, bright light was creeping in around the edges of the door she'd wedged closed with a rake, and she needed a plan. Her phone had no signal, no internet, and no GPS. She was going to have to get information the old fashioned way.

Taylor traded the trowel for the rake, and carefully opened the door. The scent of smoke hung in the air, but the backyard was empty. Snagging her bag, she made her way around the house.

Something rustled nearby and Taylor froze. She pressed herself against the brick wall of the house, heart pounding. The noise came again, accompanied by angry muttering.

Carefully, Taylor peered around the corner. A man in a store uniform was engaged in furious combat with a really big bush. He lunged at it repeatedly, grabbing handfuls of leaves and yanking them free while cursing under his breath.

"Everything is wrong," he growled at the shrubbery. "This doesn't belong here!"

Taylor watched in fascinated horror as the man attempted to pull the six-foot hedge out of the ground with his bare hands. His grip slipped and he stumbled backward, leaves flying everywhere.

Taylor wished for a moment that her phone wasn't dead so she could record this, but immediately felt guilty. This guy was obviously sick. And it wasn't like she could post it anywhere, anyway.

The hedge rustled in the breeze and he screamed at it in rage, digging his arms through the leaves to wrap his hands around the thicker interior branches. He thrashed impotently against the plant.

Taylor used his distraction to slip past, keeping close to the wall.

"Sorry about your hedge," she whispered to the absent homeowners, as she crossed the street to the high school.

In the bright morning light, Taylor examined the blank facade with a frown. She spent a large portion of every day in this building, but she'd never actually seen it completely shut down and locked up. Every window closed, every door barred. The fences around the fields and tennis courts were all chained shut and there was no sign of life anywhere.

Well, that was a dead end, she thought, sagging with exhaustion.

"Hey!"

Taylor whipped around.

A banged up minivan was barreling down the middle of the street, a woman hanging out of the window. The woman yelled again, her face contorted in rage, and Taylor ran.

Behind her tires screeched against pavement as the van jumped the curb and went bouncing across a series of well-manicured lawns. As Taylor rounded the corner there was a crash behind her.

Taylor kept running.

There were far fewer people out and about this morning, but the damage from last night was obvious. Cars sat with crumpled hoods against brick buildings or simply abandoned in the middle of intersections. Taylor paused to take stock of her surroundings. There were plumes of smoke in several directions.

She turned west and walked quickly, but carefully, her eyes scanning every street, every doorway. When Ivy's house came into view. She broke into a run when she saw the familiar structure, despite her fatigue.

There were no signs of life, but she approached cautiously, relief warring with anxiety in her chest.

Taylor knocked gently and scurried back away from the door.

"Ivy?" she called softly from the bottom of the porch steps. "It's Taylor. Please don't be crazy."

Something crashed inside the house, followed by rapid footsteps. Taylor tensed, ready to run, but her friend's face appeared in the window. Even in the dim light, Ivy's eyes were wide with fear.

The front door opened a crack, chain still in place. "What's seven times nine?"

Taylor blinked. "What?"

"Seven times nine!" Ivy's voice was shrill. "Quick!"

"Sixty-three? Ivy, what—"

The door slammed shut. The chain slid free with a clink and the door flew open to reveal Ivy brandishing what appeared to be her mother's expensive non-stick frying pan.

"Oh thank god," she breathed, lowering her makeshift weapon. "I figured if you were—" she waved the pan vaguely, "you know, infected, you wouldn't be able to do math."

"That's pretty smart," Taylor admitted. "Can I come in? I'm on the verge of a mental breakdown."

"This is so messed up." Ivy grabbed Taylor's hand to pull her into the house and slammed the door shut behind her. She wrapped Taylor in a tight hug and whispered into her shoulder, "My mom never came home last night and the guy on the radio said to stay indoors. I'm so scared."

Taylor let her bag and the rack drop to the floor to return the hug. "I'm so sorry," she whispered back. "I'm so glad you're okay. You're the first normal person I've seen since yesterday."

Ivy gave a hiccup somewhere between a laugh and a sob. "I don't feel very normal," she admitted. Pulling back, she gazed up at Taylor, who had several inches on her. "I tried calling you but none of my calls are going through. I tried to call my mom's cell phone, her office phone. I even tried to call 911," she admitted sheepishly. "I'm kind of freaking out."

"If she has what my parents had, you may be lucky that she wasn't here," Taylor said darkly. "I had to climb out of my window."

An explosion sounded from somewhere close, rocking the house, and the girls clung to each other again.

When nothing else happened, they moved to the window, craning to see any signs of whatever new disaster was unfolding.

"I don't think we should stay here," Taylor said finally. "I was thinking about trying to get to Frances's house, up the mountain road. It should be safer up there, away from town and all of the infected people."

"Yeah," Ivy agreed, wiping her eyes. "Just let me pack some stuff." She paused. "And I'm taking the frying pan."

Ten minutes later they were ready to go. Ivy had pulled her hair into a bun and changed into black leggings and a dark hoodie.

"You look like a very short cat burglar," Taylor told her.

Ivy struck a pose. "This is what I'm calling 'apocalypse chic'."

"Nice." Taylor put her hand on the doorknob. "Ready?"

Ivy raised her frying pan like a sword. "Ready."

"Your mom is going to kill you if you scratch that thing."

"Pretty sure she's got bigger problems right now." But Ivy lowered the pan slightly. "How far is it to Frances's house?"

"I think it's about four miles to the turn off and then another couple of miles up the road." Taylor pulled the door open. "Maybe a little more than that. But we can totally do it! Just think of it as conditioning for field hockey."

"Worst. Practice. Ever," Ivy muttered.

10

Tuesday Midday

After two hours of staring at my car's engine, I had accomplished exactly nothing except getting grease stains all over my favorite jeans.

There was a really good chance these were not coming out.

Those YouTube mechanics had made it look so easy—just clean the terminals, reconnect everything, and voila! But either I had forgotten some important step or there was something else seriously wrong with this car. Or it had all been clickbait.

"This is why we can't have nice things," I muttered, slamming the hood shut with a little more force than necessary. The sound echoed across the quiet mountain, making me wince. Everything seemed too loud in the un-natural stillness.

No cars on the road. No tractors in the fields. No music floating up from the drug house.

Just nothing.

"Time for Plan B," I announced to no one in particular.

Mr. Vázquez might have a landline, or maybe he'd take pity on me and drive us into town to get groceries before everything in the fridge went bad.

"Girls!" I yelled toward the house. "I'm going to check on Mr. Vázquez!"

"Whatever!" came the unified response. At least they were getting along.

I walked down to the gate, my mind busy cataloging all the ways this situation could get worse.

Power outage? Check.

Dead car? Check.

Mysterious fires in the city? Double check.

At this rate, locusts wouldn't surprise me.

I opened our gate and stepped out onto the road, my gaze wandering down to Mr. Vázquez's neat little cottage. I was halfway there when I realized there was no truck in the driveway.

Crap.

I'd come this far, so I might as well go all the way. I got to the gate and recognized the large padlock holding it shut. It was the twin to the one Mr. Vázquez had given me yesterday.

I rattled the gate, but it was locked tight.

"Hello?" I called toward the house, expectations low.

No truck, no signs of movement. The chicken man had flown the coop.

"Great," I sighed. "Just great."

Well, I'd come this far, I might as well check on Sarah and Tom. Their trailer was only another quarter mile down the road. Maybe they had a working vehicle or a landline—or some insight into what was happening in town.

The walk gave me too much time to think. I was starting to spiral as I almost walked right past their lot. The SUV was still sitting in the drive.

Thank god!

There was no lock on their gate and I threw it open and practically ran up to the trailer. I put a foot on the front step and raised my fist to knock.

The door was slightly ajar.

I froze. A chill ran down my spine and I slowly lowered my hand back down to my side.

"Hello?" I croaked out.

I cleared my throat and tried again. "Sarah? Tom?"

No response, but I could hear movement from deeper in the house. Scratching? Crying?

I pressed my fingers gently against the door and pushed it wider, my heart pounding. "It's Jane, from up the road? Your door is open..."

The living room looked normal enough, but there was a metallic smell that hung in the air and made my stomach turn.

"Oh no," I whispered, spotting the first splash of red on the wall. "No, no, no."

The crying became frantic barks.

Every horror movie I'd ever seen screamed at me to turn around and get the hell out of there, but I just couldn't. Was I really going to be that dumb bitch? The one who walks into the murder house while the audience in the theater screams at her to run?

Yes. Yes, I was.

Maybe it was the mom in me, but I couldn't leave without making sure no one needed help.

"Sarah?" I called again, much more softly this time.

The interior was set up with the kitchen to the right, which was a disaster. Stuff was strewn everywhere and an overturned chair lay in the center of a large, dark stain on the floor. On the left there was a hallway with doors leading to what I assumed were bedrooms. One of the doors shook as the dog continued to bark.

I couldn't leave the damn dog to starve to death. I crept up along the hallway toward the closed door. There were red smears on the wall and I tried not to think too hard about what might have happened here.

I hesitated for a moment. I was pretty sure this wasn't a Kujo situation, but Zeus was a really big dog. How stupid was I?

I sighed and turned the handle. Pretty stupid, was the answer.

Zeus wasn't rabid. He was, however, really happy to see me. And covered in his own shit.

"Hey, buddy," I crooned, trying not to gag at the mess he'd made of the tiny bathroom. "You're okay, Zeus. Let's get you out of here."

He didn't need to be told twice. Zeus bounded down the hallway and out the front door while I stood there trying to decide what to do. Should I search the house for clues? Try to find a phone? The keys to the SUV?

I made myself look into the two bedrooms, just to be sure. No bodies, but enough blood to make me seriously worried. The kitchen was a disaster—drawers pulled out, cabinets standing open. Signs of a struggle, or desperate packing? Also, no landline and no keys.

Zeus was waiting for me in front of the gate, pacing anxiously. When I emerged from the house, he ran over and pressed his poop-covered body against my legs like he was afraid I'd disappear.

"It's okay, buddy," I told him, patting the clean spot on the top of his head. "It's okay. Let's go."

He followed me up the road like a furry shadow, occasionally whining but never straying more than a few feet from my side. I kept looking over my shoulder, half expecting to see...something. But the road remained empty.

Hillary spotted us first. "Zeus!" she shrieked from the porch, making us both jump.

"Hills, STOP!" I screamed as she bounded down the steps.

Hillary and the dog both turned to look at me in shock.

I pointed toward the hose. "He's filthy. We have to give him a bath before anyone touches him."

Hillary skipped toward the hose as Frances appeared in the doorway. "Why do you have him? Are the neighbors okay?"

I shook my head slightly, trying to convey 'we need to talk about this later'. "They weren't there and Zeus was alone and freaking out, so we're just going to watch him for a couple of days."

Frances frowned in confusion but let it pass.

"Okay," I said, trying to sound more confident than I felt. "First things first. Hills, can you grab the unscented hand soap from under the bathroom sink and some old towels we don't care about ruining? Frances, can you grab the padlock sitting on the kitchen counter?"

"What are you going to do?" Frances asked.

"I'm going to try very hard not to have a complete mental breakdown." I managed a weak smile. "And then you guys are going to help me wash this dog."

After securing the gate, we found an old bucket in the garage and experimented with the hand pump on the well in the backyard. In no time we had water flowing. It was cold but clean.

Bathing Zeus turned out to be exactly the distraction we needed. He was surprisingly cooperative about getting wet, but had strong opinions about the soap. By the time we were done, all three of us were soaked and covered in dog hair.

"My shirt is ruined," Frances complained, wringing water out of her hair.

"Your shirt was already ruined," Hillary pointed out. "It had holes in the shoulder and ragged edges."

"It's *distressed*."

"You're distressed," Hillary shot back.

Zeus, now relatively clean and somewhat damp, sighed contentedly as I ran the towel over his big square head one last time before heaving myself to my feet.

"Inside, all of you," I ordered. "Go get changed into dry clothes and we'll figure out something for lunch."

"We should check the other houses," Frances said as we trudged through the back door and into the kitchen. "See if anyone else is still here."

"No." The word came out sharper than I intended. "No," I repeated more gently. "We need to stay here and figure out what's happening."

"But—"

"Frances." I turned to face her. "We need to be careful."

She studied my face for a moment, then nodded without asking any questions. "Okay. But we can't just stay here forever."

"I know." I pulled her into a damp hug, ignoring her token protest. "But for now, we're staying put. Together."

Hillary joined our hug, and Zeus pressed against our legs, making us all stumble.

"At least we have a guard dog now," Hillary said brightly.

I looked down at Zeus, who was rubbing his still damp body against our legs like a huge cat. "Yeah," I said dryly. "He's terrifying."

We all went upstairs to change into dry clothes. The day had warmed up, but there was still a chill in the house. I stood in my bedroom, staring at my reflection in the mirror as I pulled on a clean shirt.

"You can do this," I told myself firmly. "You've got this under control."

My reflection looked skeptical.

Walking back downstairs, I wandered into the living room and contemplated the big, ornate fireplace. Zeus, who had followed me, plopped down onto the hardwood floor in front of the empty grate.

The previous owners had left a stack of firewood on the back porch, but I'd never actually used a wood burning fireplace before. How hard could it be? Stack wood, light match, instant cozy warmth, right?

An hour later Zeus and I were both covered in soot from head to toe. It turned out that starting a fire was easy, but keeping it going required a little more finesse. It had taken a lot more effort than I'd anticipated, but the fire was dancing happily and the living room was getting nicely toasty.

"Jane Kovak, functional adult," I declared to the dog, who panted happily.

11

Tuesday Afternoon

"If this is the apocalypse, we can't just sit here and wait for the zombies to arrive," Frances argued, pacing back and forth across our living room like a caged tiger. "We need supplies. Information. Something!"

"Please don't use the Z word." I was trying for levity but it came out strained. My head was throbbing from caffeine withdrawal. "I'm not sure exactly what's going on, but we're safe here. And we have supplies."

Hillary looked up from where she was methodically sorting our pantry contents into neat piles on the table. "We have seventeen cans of cream of mushroom soup and like four thousand packets of ramen."

"See?" I gestured at the impressive wall of sodium-laden processed food. "We're set for at least a month. Or one college semester."

"Mom." Frances stopped pacing to fix me with her patented 'judgmental teenager' stare. "We need real food. And batteries. And maybe some actual information about what's happening."

"The drug dealers might know something," Hillary suggested helpfully. "They always know stuff."

I pinched the bridge of my nose and dropped down into the chair across from Frances. "We are not going to the nice drug dealers for apocalypse updates."

"Why not?" Frances demanded. "They're just down the mountain. We could walk there in like an hour."

"Because..." I struggled to articulate why this was a terrible idea without traumatizing my children. "Because it might not be safe to interact with other people right now—even non-drug dealer type people."

"Safe?" Frances threw up her hands. "Because of the virus they were talking about on TV? We've got masks." She frowned, meeting my gaze. "You think the fires and the power being out all has something to do with that GRMp thing?" She shook her head in confusion. "What exactly did you see at the neighbor's house?"

"There were signs of a struggle," I said quietly.

"A struggle?" Frances echoed. "Like from a break in? Like looters?"

"I don't think so," I muttered, dropping my head into my hands. "I think there was a fight."

"A fight?"

"There was blood, okay?" I snapped. "I think that one of them was infected and became violent and somebody got hurt. There was a lot of blood." I slammed my hands flat against the table. "Happy?"

"No! You need to be honest with us, Mom." Frances paled. "We need to know what's happening."

"*I* don't know what's happening!" My voice rose despite my best efforts to stay calm. "I don't know why the power is out or why the city is burning or what happened to our neighbors. And until I figure it out, we are staying right here!"

A sharp knock at the front door made us all jump. Zeus, who had been watching our argument like a tennis match, let out a single thunderous bark.

We all froze, staring at each other.

Another knock, more frantic this time.

"Frances? Mrs. Kovak?" A vaguely familiar voice called through the door. "Please be home!"

"That's Taylor," Frances whispered, already moving toward the door.

I caught her arm. "Wait."

"Mom!"

"Just...wait." I approached the door cautiously, Zeus at my heels. "Taylor?"

"Yes! And Ivy! Please let us in!"

"How did you guys get through the locked gate?" I asked suspiciously.

After a moment, Taylor's voice came again. "Um, we jumped your fence, ma'am. We're a little freaked out. I'm really sorry." Her voice was small through the door. "Can we please come in?"

I threw open the door to find two filthy teenagers on my porch. Taylor's shirt was torn and grimy. Ivy was clutching what appeared to be a very expensive frying pan.

"Oh thank god," Ivy breathed, and then burst into tears.

I hesitated, my hand on the knob to the storm door.

"Can we come in?" Taylor asked again, wiping a hand over her dirt-covered face.

Frances came up beside me, trying to nudge me out of the way. "Mom, let them in!"

I held my ground. "Wait."

The two girls on the porch froze and Frances turned to me with a frown.

I couldn't believe I was going to ask this. "Have you girls been infected? Do you have any symptoms?"

There was a moment when time stopped. Then Frances turned back to her friends and the four of us stared at each other through the glass of the storm door.

"No," Taylor replied firmly at the same time Ivy said, "I don't think so." They looked at each other, sharing a glance, before Taylor continued. "We've been careful. We haven't touched anyone but each other."

"No..." I let myself trail off. I couldn't bring myself to say it.

"No bite wounds?" Hillary asked from my shoulder.

"None, I swear," Taylor said, pulling up her sleeves as tears rolled silently down her cheeks.

I pushed open the screen door and they tumbled into the house. Frances joined them in a huddle as Taylor finally broke down into sobs. Eventually I was able to herd them into the kitchen, where Zeus sat at their feet, occasionally licking their hands as if to reassure himself they were real.

I made hot chocolate because that's what my mother always did in a crisis, and because I didn't know what else to do. We gathered around the kitchen table, the girls clutching their mugs like lifelines while Taylor told us what had happened.

"My parents went crazy," she said flatly. "Just completely lost it. They were fighting about the coffee maker and then they came after me. They tried to break down my bedroom door."

Frances reached across the table and squeezed her friend's hand.

"I climbed out of my window and just ran." Taylor's voice cracked. "I spent the night in someone's garden shed. It took me hours to get across town to Ivy's house."

"My mom never came home from work," Ivy added quietly. "The phones stopped working and I could hear noises outside..." She shuddered. "People were just screaming. It's like everyone was going crazy."

"Like 'zombie apocalypse' crazy," Taylor clarified. "We saw this guy try to eat a mailbox. And this woman was just walking in circles in her front yard, over and over, talking about how everything was wrong."

"They're not zombies," I protested automatically. "Zombies aren't real."

Hillary raised her hand. "Actually, Mom, the evidence suggests—"

"Let it go, Hills."

"But they are acting like zombies," Frances insisted. "Taylor's parents went crazy overnight, just like in the movies. And there was blood at Sarah and Tom's house, right?"

I sighed. "Yes, but—"

"And the city is on fire," Hillary added helpfully. "That's totally zombie movie stuff."

"Yeah," Taylor agreed. "We had to backtrack a lot on our way here because there are like whole blocks on fire."

I ran my hands through my hair in frustration. "Even if—and this is a huge if—we're dealing with some kind of infection that makes people act irrationally, that doesn't make them zombies. This isn't a movie."

"The hedge guy definitely seemed pretty zombified," Taylor muttered.

"The what now?"

"This morning I passed this guy who was trying to fight a hedge," Taylor explained. "He kept screaming at it and trying to pull it out of the ground with his bare hands."

"That's..." I trailed off, remembering the state of Sarah and Tom's kitchen. Everything pulled out of place, like someone had been frantically searching for something. Or like someone had decided everything was wrong and needed to be moved.

"Okay, that's concerning," I admitted.

"Zombies," Hillary stage-whispered.

"Not zombies," I corrected automatically. "But definitely something we need to be careful about." I looked at Taylor and Ivy's exhausted faces. "You girls can stay here as long as you need to. We'll figure this out together."

"Thanks, Mrs. Kovak." Ivy gave me a wan smile. "Sorry about coming over without calling first. Again."

I surprised myself by laughing. "Well, at least this time you didn't try to summon demons in my treehouse."

"We were doing homework," Frances protested.

"Yeah." Taylor managed a small grin. "Usually we confine the human sacrifice to the basement."

"As long as you clean up after yourselves," I said dryly. "Now, who wants to help me figure out how to heat water in the fireplace? I am *not* living through an apocalypse without caffeine. And no, Hillary, we are not calling it a *'zombie'* apocalypse."

"Yet," Hillary muttered, but she got up to help anyway.

As I watched the girls jury-rig a hook for my old kettle over the fire, I tried not to think too hard about what Taylor and Ivy had said. Whatever was happening in town was real and it was spreading. We weren't just waiting out a power outage anymore.

We were hiding from something much worse.

Zeus pressed against my leg and I reached down to scratch his ears. "Good boy," I murmured. "At least someone around here isn't trying to convince me we're living in a George Romero movie."

The dog wagged his tail and licked my hand.

"Though I have to admit," I added quietly, "the evidence is mounting."

12

Tuesday Evening

Hector

F ires dotted the city skyline and Hector hadn't slept in three days. His eyes were dry and hot, like sandy raisins rolling around in his head.

"Dispatch, Unit 247 responding to shots fired at Monroe Park," he called an update into his radio for what felt like the hundredth time that night.

Only static answered.

He navigated his patrol bike around abandoned vehicles, the thick tires easily rolling over the rubble and trash that dotted the asphalt. Some idiot had abandoned their ugly electric truck right in the middle of Broad Street. The charging stations had gone down with the grid. The only light on the street now was from the moon and the fires.

A group of people ran past him, and in the dark he couldn't tell if they were running from the infected or if they were the infected. The distinction was getting harder to make. The virus—or whatever it was—had gotten completely out of control.

Hector stopped his bike and looked over his shoulder at the group, frozen with indecision.

Another shot rang out ahead of him and he whipped around to squint through the darkness.

Ted would have known what to do. But Ted was probably dead, along with most of their precinct. The hospital had become a death trap when the power failed and the backup generators didn't kick in. The infected had broken containment and the entire area went under lockdown.

Hector shook his head. He couldn't think about that now.

His radio crackled to life. "Any units in the vicinity of VCU Medical Center, we have civilians barricaded in the pharmacy. Multiple hostiles outside."

"Dispatch? This is Unit 247, I'm about ten minutes out," Hector responded, relief flooding through him at hearing another human voice.

"Negative, 247. Stand down. The National Guard is handling all medical center calls."

Hector snorted. "With all due respect, dispatch, the National Guard is currently shooting anything that moves."

"Shelter in place, 247," the voice insisted. "And await further instructions."

Hector gazed at the radio, torn. Should he try to make his way back to his apartment? Still undecided, Hector started pedaling forward again, taking the first right to head west toward his neighborhood.

A woman stumbled into the street in front of him, and he slammed on the brakes, his feet hitting the asphalt hard. She turned toward him, and he tensed, hand moving to his weapon. Her eyes were wide and bloodshot, but clear.

"Officer! Please, you have to help! My daughter..." She collapsed onto the ground, sobbing.

Hector checked up and down the block, before cautiously getting off his bike. "Ma'am, where is your daughter?"

"In our apartment, three blocks that way." She pointed east. "She's diabetic, and we're out of insulin. The pharmacy—I tried, but—"

"Show me," he said, helping her up. "What's your name?"

"Maria." She grasped his hand in relief, the tears on her face glinting under the moonlight. "Thank you, thank you."

"Don't thank me yet," Hector muttered, grabbing his bike by the handlebars to walk it back the way he'd come. "Which building?"

Maria pointed, clutching at his hand like a lifeline. "The Madison, apartment 4C. My husband went for help yesterday and he never came back."

Hector's jaw tightened. He'd seen too many similar stories in the past days. People trying to help their loved ones, only to become victims themselves. Richmond was a giant maze now, with some routes blocked by the infected and others by National Guard checkpoints. Neither were particularly friendly.

They reached the apartment building without incident, which immediately made Hector suspicious. Nothing had been this easy since Saturday.

"Stay behind me," he instructed Maria as they entered the lobby.

The emergency lights cast an eerie red glow over everything.

"The elevators aren't working," Maria said, heading for the stairs.

Four flights up, Hector was grateful for all those morning runs with his police academy buddies. Maria was wheezing behind him, but she didn't complain.

The fourth floor hallway was silent. Too silent.

Hector drew his weapon. "Which apartment?"

"The last one on the left." Maria moved past him, reaching for her keys.

A crash came from nearby, followed by a high-pitched scream.

"Amy!" Maria lunged forward, but Hector caught her arm.

"Wait," he commanded. "Is there anyone else who should be in there?"

She shook her head, tears streaming down her face.

"Stay here." He approached the door carefully, testing the handle. Locked.

Another crash. Hector tilted his head, trying to figure out which apartment it was coming from.

Maria thrust her keys at him with shaking hands. Hector inserted the key as quietly as possible, but the lock's click seemed to echo in the silent hallway.

He pushed the door open slowly, weapon ready. The apartment was dark except for sunlight filtering through partially closed blinds.

Something moved in his peripheral vision. He spun, catching a glimpse of a small figure darting into the kitchen.

"Amy?" he called out softly. "I'm a police officer. I'm here to help."

A sob came from behind the kitchen island, followed by rapid breathing.

"Where's my mom?" The voice was young, frightened.

"She's right outside, sweetheart. Are you hurt?"

"No."

Hector holstered his weapon and pulled out his flashlight. "I'm going to come around the counter now, okay?"

He found a little girl of about six or seven huddled in the corner, hugging her knees. Her face was pale and drawn, but her eyes were clear.

"Hi Amy, I'm a police officer. My name is Hector. Your mom says you need insulin?"

She nodded weakly.

"Maria?" he called out. "It's clear."

Maria rushed in, gathering her daughter in her arms. "Baby, I'm so sorry I was gone so long. Did you check your sugar?"

"The meter's dead," Amy mumbled into her mother's shoulder. "But I feel really bad."

Hector was already moving, checking the rest of the small apartment.

"It's clear, but you can't stay here," he told them as Maria helped Amy to her feet. "The hospital's overrun, but there's a shelter set up in the high school. They have medical staff and supplies."

Maria nodded, already gathering essentials into a backpack. "Amy, can you walk?"

The girl was shaky, but standing. "I think so."

They made it back to the street and Hector looked at his bike with regret. Walking past it, he approached a little black hatchback parked on the side of the street. Within minutes he had the car running, relieved to see a half tank of gas.

Maria looked on with a frown. "We're stealing it?"

"Commandeering," he corrected. "Get in the back and keep your heads down."

Hector drove slowly, weaving his way through the streets. They'd only gone a couple of blocks when his radio crackled again, making them all jump.

"All units, be advised. Command structure is compromised. All units switch to emergency protocol alpha."

"What does that mean?" Maria asked from the backseat, where she was holding Amy.

Hector's mouth was set in a grim line. "It means we're on our own." He met her eyes in the rearview mirror. "Help isn't coming."

The rest of the drive to the shelter was tense. Hector doubled back to avoid the sounds of shots, and twice they had to make quick detours to avoid roaming packs of the infected.

The high school was at the end of a cul-de-sac and surrounded by a high brick wall. A mixed group of armed men and women stood at the gate. Most of them seemed to be civilians but Hector recognized a friendly face as they rolled up slowly in the stolen car.

"Clemens!" Hector called.

The uniform stepped forward, squinting through the open window. "Hector?" She waved the other guards back. "Jesus, man. What are you still doing on the street?"

She turned away without waiting for an answer and waved her arm. The gate began to slowly move back.

"Park that thing on the left side. You guys got the last three beds," she told him as she waved the three of them through. "We're at capacity now."

Hector followed her directions and within minutes a nurse was checking Amy's vitals. Hector stood in the doorway, watching, as Clemens came up to stand at his shoulder.

"I'm not staying," he said softly. "I've got to get back out there."

She shrugged. "Your funeral, man. Half the force is either dead or AWOL and the National Guard just abandoned its checkpoints. The infection rate is exponential now." She ran a hand through her short hair. "At least our generator is still running."

There was a loud thunk from the building behind her and the lights perched at the top of the wall flickered and died.

"You brought that on yourself," Hector snickered while she cursed.

Hector worked on their generator for most of the night to no avail, before grabbing a couple of hours of sleep on their last cot. The sun was just peeking between the buildings as he drove away from the shelter, painting the sky in shades of red.

13

Wednesday Morning

"We're going to die of sodium poisoning," Frances announced, pulling more packets of ramen noodles from the pantry.

"Is that a thing?" Ivy asked.

"Actually," Hillary piped up from her perch on the counter, "I once read that in a survival situation, extra sodium can be beneficial."

"Nobody is dying of sodium poisoning," I interrupted, trying to sound confident. "Or any other kind of poisoning. We have plenty of options," I lied, peered into a mostly empty cabinet.

"Zeus thinks the Cream of mushroom soup is delicious," Hillary pointed out. She hopped down off of the counter and patted the dog on his big, square head, picking his empty bowl up from the floor.

"It isn't really breakfast food," Taylor pointed out unhelpfully from the floor, where she and Ivy were tackling the lower cabinets. Her upper body was mostly inside a cabinet and her voice was muffled.

"Not with that attitude, it isn't." I closed the cabinet I'd been rummaging through and leaned against the counter. "Look, we just need to be creative. Think outside the box. Way outside the box. Like, possibly in a completely different box adjacent to the original box."

"Or," Hillary suggested brightly, "we could catch some chickens!"

"No."

"But Mom—"

"We are not eating the demon chickens." *Not yet, at least.* I pulled out a package of stale crackers and some peanut butter. "Here. Protein."

Taylor's head emerged from the cabinet and she pushed herself to her feet, brushing dust off of a pair of Frances' sweatpants she'd borrowed. I passed her the package of crackers and she squinted at it suspiciously.

"These expired three years ago," she noted, unhelpfully.

"That's just a suggestion," I assured her. "Like recommended speeds on curves and off ramps."

Frances snorted. "Yeah, that's not what the police officer said when you got that ticket."

"It was only a warning," I corrected.

"Because you cried."

"I had something in my eye." I brandished a peanut butter-covered butter knife in a threatening manner. "Now eat your breakfast before I forget I'm supposed to be the responsible adult in this situation."

The four girls settled around the kitchen table, making various noises of protest as they spread expired peanut butter on stale crackers. I tried not to think about how quickly we were going through our supplies or what we'd do when they ran out.

Do you pluck chickens before frying them?

A knock at the door made us all freeze. Zeus, who had slunk under the table, hoping someone would drop a cracker, lifted his head and barked.

"Stay here," I told the girls, grabbing the baseball bat I'd left by the door for exactly this purpose.

I peered through the peephole. "Oh thank god," I breathed, lowering my improvised weapon. "It's Mr. Vázquez."

I opened the door to find our elderly neighbor looking considerably more disheveled than I'd ever seen him. His usually neat clothing was wrinkled and there were dark shadows under his eyes.

"Buenos días," he said softly, holding out a basket full of eggs and potatoes.

"Oh," I said stupidly. "Oh, my god." I opened the storm door and wrapped my arms around the basket. "Hillary!" I called over my shoulder. "I need your Spanish skills!"

Hillary bounded to the door, followed by the rest of the girls and Zeus. "Hi, Mr. Vázquez!"

He smiled briefly at her before launching into what seemed like a very serious explanation, complete with dramatic hand gestures.

Hillary's face scrunched up in concentration. "He's saying there are Los Muertos in the town." She turned to look at me, her expression serious for once. "Dead people."

Mr. Vázquez nodded vigorously and made a shambling motion with his arms.

Her eyes went wide. "I think he's talking about zombies!"

"Hills, I'm sure that's not—"

But Mr. Vázquez was nodding again, pointing toward town and making more animated gestures. "Muy peligroso," he said seriously, continuing with more Spanish.

"He says it's dangerous," Hillary translated. "We need to stay up here on the mountain. Stay together. Be careful."

Our neighbor mimed locking a door, then pointed at his eyes and gestured around us.

"Gracias," I told him sincerely, still hugging the basket of food to my chest. "Por favor, stay safe."

He touched my arm briefly and turned to head back down our driveway. There was a faint jingle as he unlocked our gate and relocked it after himself. I wasn't one hundred percent sure I was comfortable knowing that he'd kept a key to the padlock he'd given us, but I guess it made sense. Something to think about later.

I'd add it to the list.

"Well," I said to break the heavy silence. "Who wants some real breakfast?"

While I made eggs, the girls brainstormed ways to reinforce the fence around the property. Apparently they'd been watching the chickens escape through various holes and had some ideas about patching them.

"It's not just about the chickens anymore," Frances pointed out.

"Zombies," Hillary clarified helpfully.

"Don't—" I stopped myself with a sigh. "You know what? Fine. Zombie-proof fencing it is. But we work together and everyone stays where I can see them."

We spent the morning patching holes and reinforcing weak spots with wire from the garage. The previous owners had let the fence fall into disrepair, but with five pairs of hands, we made good progress. Frances and I were finishing up the front section and I sent the other girls to start on the back, under Zeus' careful supervision.

I was standing on the outside of the fence, hammering the last loose board back into place, when a familiar engine roar made me look up. Clyde's massive truck thundered past our gate, going way too fast. He didn't even slow down to glare at us.

"Gee," Frances commented from where she was threading wire through fence post from the other side. "I guess he isn't going to stop to threaten legal action."

"Maybe he finally found Jesus," I snarked.

I turned to make another smartass comment and froze.

Tom was standing in the middle of the road. His clothes were torn and bloody, his skin paper white and his eyes blood red.

"Frances," I said very quietly. "Get in the house."

Tom's head snapped up at the sound of my voice and he let out an inhuman growl.

"Now!" I screamed, as he lunged for me.

I swung the hammer up instinctively and caught him in the shoulder.

He didn't even seem to notice, just kept coming. His hands were reaching for my throat and his teeth were snapping and *oh god this wasn't happening*.

I swung the hammer at his head and it connected with a sickening crack.

Tom dropped to the ground and didn't move.

I turned to find all four girls standing frozen on the porch, Zeus growling beside them.

"Inside," I repeated hoarsely. "All of you. Now."

They scrambled to obey as I stared down at Tom's still body, the hammer dangling from my shaking hands.

"Well," I said to no one in particular, "I guess Hillary was right about the zombies."

Then I threw up in the rose bushes.

14

Wednesday Midday

Hector

Hector swung open the door to his apartment and a folded piece of paper fluttered to the floor. He scooped it up as his eyes scanned the small space.

At first glance the apartment was exactly as he'd left it on Saturday morning—dishes in the sink and half-empty coffee cup on the table. In the kitchen, the loaf of bread he'd left on the counter had been reduced to crumbs and a few strips of plastic.

"Enjoy," he muttered to whatever rodent had gone to town during his absence, and opened up the note.

Hector stood silently, absorbing the words written in his father's angular scrawl. It wasn't dated, but his father had obviously been here at some point in the last three days.

Hector cursed softly and without any real heat. There was no way he could have known that his father would come here—or exactly when. Hector couldn't have sat here waiting, while people were being hurt and killed in the city.

Walking into his bedroom, Hector refolded the note and slipped it into his pocket. He grabbed his go bag from the back of the door and threw it onto the bed. To the bag he added extra ammunition, his backup piece, and a box of protein bars that his furry invader had left untouched.

The power was out but the water was still running so he filled several bottles and wedged them into the pack. His father always said water was worth more than gold in a crisis. His father had said a lot of things that had seemed paranoid at the time, but made a lot of sense right now.

The drive to his dad's house would normally take about four hours, but the roads were a mess. The infected had a very bad habit of driving their cars into buildings. And pedestrians. Hector shook his head. It had been a rough three days.

He grabbed his leather jacket from the hook by the door and made his way down to the building's parking lot. His SUV sat in its usual spot. The four wheel drive might have come in handy, but the vehicle wasn't ideal for navigating the maze the city had become.

And the tank was almost empty.

Hector silently cursed his past self. Sighing, he switched his gaze to his neighbor's parking spot and the big, muscular motorcycle parked there.

"Sorry," Hector said to the bike's absent owner as he hot wired the ignition. "But you're not using it and I need a ride out of town."

He slipped on his sunglasses and rolled the bike out of the parking lot. A helmet would have been nice, but at this point a head injury was pretty far down the list of things he was worried about.

Richmond looked like something out of a disaster movie. His neighborhood was strewn with debris and smoke rose from almost every block. The occasional burst of gunfire echoed down the streets. Hector passed a Starbucks with its windows smashed and thought of the Karen from last week. He hoped she'd found her Venti in hell.

Getting out of the city was a challenge. The National Guard had blockaded most major routes, and the back streets were a maze of abandoned vehicles and wandering infected.

Hector was cutting through a residential area when he heard screams. A minivan was wrapped around a street light, its front end crumpled. A man was trying to extract a car seat from the back while a woman fought off two infected with a baseball bat.

"Goddammit," Hector muttered, bringing the bike to a stop. He couldn't just leave them.

The woman was holding her own, but the man's hands were shaking so badly he couldn't get the car seat unclipped. The woman took one of the attackers to the ground, beating it into submission. As the other came up behind her, arms outstretched, Hector took it out with a clean shot through the forehead.

The woman didn't react, continuing to rail into the zombie she'd brought down.

Hector ran over to the van. "I'm a cop. Let me help," he told the man, using a gentle hand on his shoulder to move him out of the way. In seconds Hector had the crying child unbuckled. He was a big baby, or a small toddler, and was solid under Hector's hands as he lifted him out of the seat and passed him to his trembling father.

"Thank you," the man gasped out, maneuvering the baby into a front carrier. "Those things came out of nowhere and we went right into the pole." Baby settled into place, the cries became tired sniffles. "We're trying to make it to my sister-in-law's place in Virginia Beach."

Hector shook his head. "Virginia Beach is gone," he said quietly. "Try heading west instead. The infection's spreading slower in the mountains."

The woman finally stopped pounding on the infected at her feet and her head snapped in their direction.

Her eyes were red.

Hector backed slowly toward his bike. "Listen to me carefully," he said calmly, without moving his gaze from the woman. "Your wife is infected."

The man spun around, horror dawning across his face. "Amber?" he asked, his voice breaking.

He raised a hand toward her and she brought her bat down hard into the road, asphalt spraying in every direction.

"No, no, no!" she cried out, striking the ground again and again.

Hector got onto his bike and started the engine. "Get on."

"Amber?" the man said, reluctantly backing away from the spray of gravel. His baby had started crying again. "Please, Amber."

"This is your last chance," Hector said, hardening his heart. "Get on and I'll take you and your kid somewhere safe." Hector shrugged. "Or safer, at least. But if I stay here any longer, I'm going to have to shoot her."

Tears running down his face, the man swung a leg over the bike and settled into the seat behind Hector. With the baby and the backpack between them, it was awkward, but Hector pulled out slowly, the sound of the baseball bat hitting the street fading behind them.

The sun was setting by the time Hector pulled off into a small campground just off Route 60, far enough from the road to avoid attention but close enough to hear approaching vehicles. He'd learned to sleep light these past few days, catching rest in short bursts between the screams and gunfire.

There were two campsites set up but both appeared deserted. Hector pulled the bike to a stop in front of one and waited for his passengers to dismount before swinging his leg over the bike. After getting the heavy machine set onto its kickstand, he turned and extended a hand.

"Hector," he said, as the younger man accepted the handshake.

"I'm Ryan," he replied, beginning to unbuckle the carrier holding his sleeping child. "This is Joey." Ryan stared down at his son's quiet face then glanced up at Hector. "Thank you."

Hector nodded, pulling his weapon as he carefully lifted the flap of the nearest tent. "I'm sorry about your wife."

The interior of the tent was empty except for abandoned camping gear—two sleeping bags, a lantern, and a half-empty pack of trail mix. Hector checked the other tent, finding similar supplies. He grabbed the food and a flashlight and returned to the first tent, waving Ryan inside.

"We can use these," he said, gathering the gear into a pile. "You should get some rest."

Ryan settled Joey into one of the sleeping bags, the baby barely stirring. In the fading light, Hector could see the man's hands were still shaking.

"Where are we going?" Ryan asked quietly, his gaze still on his sleeping son.

Hector settled down on the other bag. "My dad's place. We should make it there tomorrow."

"I keep seeing her face," Ryan whispered. "Her eyes." He broke off, covering his face with his hands.

Hector pulled out two protein bars, offering one to Ryan. "Is there anywhere else you can go, besides Virginia Beach?"

"Not really." Ryan took the bar but didn't open it. "Amber was really irritable last night. I thought it was just stress, you know? Everyone's been on edge with all the news reports." He looked toward the tent where Joey slept. "What am I going to tell him when he's older?"

"Tell him his mother fought to protect him until the very end," Hector said firmly. "That's all he needs to know."

15

Still Wednesday, Maybe

I'd always imagined the zombie apocalypse would involve more dramatic speeches about humanity's survival and less sitting on the bathroom floor having existential crises. But here I was, hyperventilating into a paper bag while the girls played with glitter glue.

"Mom!" Hillary's voice carried through the door. "Come see what we made!"

"Just a minute!" I called back, trying to sound normal and not like someone who had recently murdered their neighbor. Former neighbor.

Zombified neighbor? What was the proper terminology here?

I had deaded the undead.

I caught my reflection in the mirror and immediately regretted it. "You look like someone who killed a zombie with a hammer," I told myself. "Pull it together, Jane."

My reflection remained unconvinced.

"Mom!" This time it was Frances. "Stop having a breakdown and come take our picture!"

"I'm not having a breakdown," I muttered, opening the door. "I'm having a perfectly reasonable reaction to an unreasonable situation."

The girls were clustered around the front door, where Hillary had erected what looked like a crossing guard sign covered in glitter. The words "NO GRMPIES!!!" were written in sparkly pink letters, accompanied by what I assumed was supposed to be a threatening skull.

"The virus is GRMp," Hillary explained proudly. "So they're Grumpies!"

"That's..." I searched for the right words. "Really catchy, Hills."

"Take our picture!" Taylor thrust her phone at me.

I accepted the phone automatically and stared down at the illuminated screen blankly. "How does your phone still have a charge?"

There was no signal, but the thing was definitely still working.

I looked up at Taylor in amazement. "My phone has been dead for days."

"I have a solar charger in my bag." She gestured vaguely toward the house. "For camping."

"You packed a solar charger but not a change of clothes?"

She shrugged. "Priorities."

"Huh." I shrugged. "Can't argue with that." I lined up the shot as the girls posed dramatically in front of Hillary's sign. "Say 'brains'!"

"Mom!" Frances protested, but she was laughing.

"Too soon?"

I took several photos while the girls struck increasingly ridiculous poses. When we were done I handed Taylor back her phone and asked to borrow her charger later. We wandered back into the house, the girls relaxed and happy.

"I should check on the drug house," I muttered, hating to break the mood. I definitely didn't want to trudge down there, but it was the right thing to do. Probably.

"See if they've talked to Mr. Vázquez," I added. "Make sure they know what's happening and see if they need help."

"Can we come?" Hillary asked hopefully.

"Absolutely not." I called Zeus over. "You four stay inside the house and work on your zombie apocalypse scrapbook or whatever."

"Journal," Taylor corrected. "We're documenting historical events."

"With glitter," Ivy added.

I left them arguing over proper scrapbooking techniques, resigned to finding glitter embedded in my house for the next ten years. In the garage I dug out an old baseball bat, and headed down the mountain with Zeus by my side.

We passed Mr. Vázquez's house, his pickup truck now parked outside. Zeus paused at the gate to Tom and Sarah's, but trotted after me when I called him. Everything was eerily quiet except for the occasional distant explosion from town.

We were halfway to the drug house when I spotted movement at the side of the road. A man, covered in dirt and tattered clothing was wandering aimlessly through the brush at the bottom of a ditch, occasionally stopping to pull up plants and throw them. The drop off was only about three feet, but the man—the zombie—seemed firmly stuck.

Zeus growled low in his throat.

"Shh," I whispered, moving to the far side of the road. I tightened my grip on the bat and picked up our speed. "Good boy. Just stay quiet."

The drug house looked abandoned. There were only two cars in the driveway and someone had nailed boards across the windows.

As we walked up to the front of the house, there was a pile of empty beer cans functioning as a makeshift alarm system across the steps.

I leaned over the cans and reached out with the bat to knock carefully on the door. "Hello? It's your neighbor from up the road!"

There were a series of crashes and curses before the door opened a crack, revealing a tall, thin guy in his mid twenties.

"Oh thank fuck," he said, pulling the door wider. "We thought you were a zombie."

"Not yet." I leaned over the can barricade gingerly, taking in the chaos of the interior. The place looked like it had been ransacked. "Although the day is young."

"Shit." He ran a hand through his greasy hair. "Yeah, people are going crazy everywhere. We've been hiding out here, but we're out of...everything."

There were two other young men in their early to mid twenties sprawled across a long, low couch in the living room. A girl with stringy red hair was curled in an over-stuffed chair, shaking.

"Lucy's not feeling great. None of us are," he explained quietly. "We're gonna have to make a run into town."

"That's a terrible idea."

"You got a better one?"

I didn't. "Have you heard anything? We're not getting any signals and the power is out."

"Timmy and Mikey said they saw army guys." He gestured toward one of the guys draped across the sofa.

"Hey." The guy fluttered his fingers our way without any other signs of movement. "I'm Mike. That's a really big dog."

I waved back. "I'm Jane, from up the hill. This is Zeus. You saw army guys? Like the U.S. Army?" I prompted.

Mike shrugged. "I guess? They were in Richmond."

"Not in town?"

"It was dark by the time we made it to town and we couldn't really see anything." Mike shrugged again, apparently the extent of his mobility.

"Well." I turned back to the guy still holding the door open. "Just be careful if you go into town, I guess."

"No shit." He glanced around. "But we can't just sit here and wait them out. We'll fucking die."

Would you, though? I tried not to stare at the shivering girl.

"Well, good luck!" I said with a cheery smile, backing Zeus down the steps.

We headed back up the mountain, my mind spinning with scenarios. The zombie was right where we'd left him, and we clung to the opposite side of the road to make it past—which is why we weren't killed when Clyde's truck came barreling around the corner behind us, blaring music.

I lurched to the side as the wake of the truck blew my hair across my face. Zeus stumbled into my legs and I cartwheeled my arms to keep my balance. I lost my bat.

"Holy shit," I gasped out, pushing my hair back and reaching down to pat the big dog trembling at my feet. "You're okay, buddy."

The truck had stopped about fifty feet away, a cloud of dirt swirling between us.

I was dusting off my pants with shaky hands when the truck slammed into reverse and rolled back toward us. It came way too close, testing my bladder's fortitude, before skidding to a stop and spewing dirt and gravel back over me and Zeus, who started barking.

"Hey!" I yelled over Zeus's barking and the unintelligible country rock anthem that was still playing at an eardrum-splitting level. "What the hell is wrong with you?"

The volume of the music decreased and Clyde leaned out of the driver side window with a wide grin, showing way too many teeth.

"Just providing some entertainment for our new friends," he announced.

"What?" I stared at him in confusion, shushing Zeus with a hand on his back. "You're playing music for the zombies?"

"They really like it." He adjusted the speaker down again. "It's hilarious watching them try to chase me."

I stared at him. "Are you insane? You're going to get us all killed."

"Lighten up, little lady." He winked at me and reached onto the seat beside him. Lifting some kind of rifle into view, he winked and said, "Think of it as population control."

Zeus growled, low and threatening.

Clyde's smile dropped. "That's not your dog."

"He is now," I replied firmly, placing a hand on Zeus' tall back.

Clyde's frown twisted into a sneer. "Then you'd better keep him under control."

"And you'd better keep your music down," I countered. "Unless you want to explain to the police why you're deliberately endangering people."

"Ain't no police anymore, honey," Clyde scoffed. "You need protection, you come on up to the top of the mountain. I'll keep you safe, sugar." He winked and turned the music back up. His tires spun for a second and then he peeled off, back up the mountain, leaving us in a cloud of dirt and exhaust.

I picked up my bat and rubbed Zeus across the top of his big head. We walked home in blessed silence, and my hands had stopped shaking by the time we made it to our gate. The girls must have been plastered to the window, because they all tumbled out onto the porch to greet us.

"How was the drug house?" Frances asked as I climbed the steps.

"About what you'd expect." I set my bat by the door and collapsed into a porch chair. "And I ran into Zombie Apocalypse Clyde—who is shockingly even more annoying than regular Clyde."

"Just another Tuesday in the apocalypse," Taylor said cheerfully.

"It's Thursday," Ivy corrected her.

Frances frowned. "I'm pretty sure it's Wednesday."

"Time is meaningless now," Hillary declared. "We measure days in zombie encounters."

I looked at their excited faces and felt a wave of completely inappropriate laughter building. "So on a scale of one to 'killing your neighbor with a hammer', how's everyone's day going?"

"Mom!" Frances sounded scandalized, but she was fighting a smile.

"Still too soon?"

16

Thursday, Probably

Hector

Hector slowed the motorcycle as they passed the town's welcome sign, across the bottom of which someone had helpfully spray painted "to hell".

"Charming," he muttered, carefully navigating around an overturned pickup truck.

The small town had clearly seen better days. Rhythmic banging grew louder as they passed the elementary school and Ryan's fingers tightened where they clutched at the back of Hector's jacket. Every window in the building was shattered. Small figures scattered throughout the playground were raising and lowering various sports equipment and garden tools in unison against the metal slides and swings. They lifted hockey sticks and rakes high over their heads and brought them down, again and again.

"Are those...?" Ryan started.

"Don't look," Hector advised. "At least they aren't fighting."

Main Street was a disaster zone. The hardware store's front window was shattered, tools and supplies scattered across the sidewalk. There were abandoned cars everywhere, many embedded into buildings and light poles. The double doors to the diner were hanging askew, showcasing overturned tables and broken chairs.

A woman in a postal uniform was walking down the street, methodically smashing windows with what appeared to be someone's prosthetic leg. She didn't look up as they drove past, focused on her destruction of property.

There was a gas station in the next block, a battered minivan sticking out of the front window of the attached convenience store. The bike's tank was hovering near empty, so Hector pulled up to one of the pumps. It was dead, the digital display dark.

"We need to find gas before we head up the mountain," he told Ryan, killing the engine. "Keep your eyes open while I check these cars."

The small parking lot held several vehicles but the doors were locked, along with the gas tank access. The minivan wedged into the storefront, however, was standing with its doors wide open. Hector maneuvered carefully through the space between the side of the vehicle and the broken glass.

Once inside the store, he grabbed a red plastic gas can from a shelf and pulled a length of hose from the back of one of the freezers. Within minutes he was siphoning gas into the can.

"Incoming," Ryan warned softly from where he stood cradling Joey in his carrier near the rear of the van.

Hector glanced up to see a large man in a security guard uniform lumbering down the sidewalk, dragging a shovel behind him. Blood stained his shirt front.

"Almost done," Hector muttered, working faster.

The infected guard was moving slowly, probably due to what looked like a nasty wound on his leg.

The metal end of the shovel scraped loudly along the concrete sidewalk, causing the baby to stir and whimper.

"Shh, buddy," Ryan soothed, bouncing slightly. "Just a little longer."

The guard's head snapped toward the sound.

Hector pulled the hose free. The can was filled maybe half-way, but it was better than nothing. He passed the container to Ryan then climbed through the gap.

"Get on the bike," he said calmly.

Ryan moved directly to the bike while Hector cut an arched path to keep himself between them and the infected. Reluctantly, he pulled his service weapon. He had limited ammunition, and perhaps even more importantly, he'd rather not draw any more attention. He'd figured out that the infected were at their most violent when disturbed by loud noises. He and Ryan had been surprisingly successful in avoiding trouble up to this point.

Apparently their luck had run out.

Just as Ryan swung his leg over the bike, the guard lunged forward with surprising speed, swinging his shovel. Hector stepped up and caught the blow on his forearm and kicked out, sending the infected man sprawling.

"Time to go!" He holstered his weapon and slid behind the handlebars.

They peeled away from the station, Joey and the gas can wedged awkwardly between them, as the guard scrambled to his feet. He snapped his teeth in their direction but didn't try to run after them.

Once they were clear of the town, Hector picked a quiet spot to stop and emptied the can into the tank. They continued along the two lane road out of town for another ten minutes or so before Hector brought the bike to a stop at the bottom of the mountain road.

"This is it," he called over his shoulder.

"Your dad lives up there?" Ryan asked.

"Yeah." Hector smiled, putting the bike back into gear. "His farm is about two thirds up this private road. He bought this place after my mom died when he decided he didn't want to talk to people anymore."

There were goats roaming behind the fence at the little cottage at the end of the road, but no people visible. Hector thought about stopping, but he was so close now, he needed to see his dad. Using caution on the old road, he started them up the mountain.

The next house they passed seemed abandoned, a modern monstrosity with boarded windows and no signs of life. Another mile up the mountain there was a cute little mobile home with an SUV sitting out front, looking completely undisturbed.

"Should we stop?" Ryan asked in his ear.

Hector just shook his head. They could investigate later.

His dad's little cottage came into view, with a familiar old pickup sitting in the drive. As the bike pulled up in front of the house, the door flew open and all of the tension in Hector's chest released. Tears welled behind his sunglasses as Luis Vázquez raced down the porch steps.

Hector barely had time to bring the bike to a stop before his father was pulling him into a crushing hug.

"*Gracias a Dios*!" Luis exclaimed, clutching his son to his barrel chest. "When you weren't in your apartment, I feared the worst."

"I found your note," Hector told him, pulling back to look his dad up and down. "I came as soon as I could. You're okay?"

"I am now, *hijo*," Luis laughed, his eyes shining with tears. Glancing over Hector's shoulder, Luis eyed his passengers. "And who have you brought me?"

Hector turned to gesture them forward. "This Ryan and his son Joey." He raised his eyebrows at his father. "I thought you might have room for them." He lowered his voice. "Ryan's wife..." Hector let his voice trail off and just shook his head.

"Of course!" Luis interjected. "Come, Ryan. It is very nice to meet you and your handsome son."

He pulled a somewhat shellshocked Ryan into a hug. Joey, still in the carrier, giggled between them.

"Thank you for keeping my son company on his trip." Wrapping an arm around both men, Luis began ushering them into the house. "You must tell me everything."

There was movement at the farmhouse further up the road and Hector turned in growing amazement as a flurry of girls and a huge brown dog poured out into the yard.

Luis waved his arm over his head. "Jane! *Chicas*, you must come and meet my son!"

As the girls came tumbling out of their gate and rushed down the road, Hector realized one of them was an actual adult woman. She held a baseball bat in one hand and pushed her way in front of the teenagers, fluttering her free hand at them to keep them back.

She stared at Luis in amazement. "I'm sorry, what?"

17
Definitely Thursday

"I'm sorry, what?" I blurted out.

I let the tip of my trusty bat rest against the road as I stared at Mr. Vásquez, who was grinning at me without a trace of guilt. "You speak English?"

"Only when I have to," he replied cheerfully, leaning down to pet Zeus.

I opened and closed my mouth several times, trying to process this information.

"Hillary's Spanish is very good," he assured me. "Though perhaps we should work on her accent."

"You understood me this whole time!" I accused.

Behind him, his son—who had luscious wavy dark hair and a good six inches on his father—was trying unsuccessfully to hide his laughter. His dark eyes twinkled, which just made me more irritated.

"I find people are less likely to engage in small talk if they think there's a language barrier," Mr. Vásquez explained reasonably.

"That's..." I stopped, considering. "Actually brilliant," I admitted in defeat.

"Gracias!" Luis beamed.

"No," I corrected. "Thank you. For the pomegranates and the potatoes and everything." I waved helplessly. "And the padlock. Thank you for looking out for us, Mr. Vásquez." I met his gaze, ignoring the stinging at the corners of my own eyes.

Stupid allergies.

"That is what neighbors are for," he said gently. "And please, call me Luis. Now, let me introduce my son, Hector, and his..." he gestured vaguely at the man holding the toddler.

"Partner?" I supplied helpfully.

The son—Hector—choked on air while the other man turned bright red.

"N-no," he stammered. "We just met. Hector saved us from zombies."

"How romantic," I deadpanned.

Hillary bounded forward before anyone could correct me further. "Can I hold your baby?" she asked, peering at the sleeping child. "What's his name? I'm really good with babies. I've never dropped one."

"Hillary," I interrupted, "maybe introduce yourself before demanding to hold people's babies?"

"I'm Hillary," my youngest announced proudly. "I'm eight and I know how to make a flamethrower."

He clutched his child closer to his chest.

"She absolutely does not know how to make a flamethrower," I assured him. Then, under my breath, "I hope."

"My name is Taylor and I haven't dropped a baby either!" Taylor chimed in. "Not even once!"

"That's because you've never held one," Frances pointed out.

"I have, too. I have baby cousins and I babysit all the time." Taylor waved this off. "I'm very responsible."

"You set fire to your math homework," Ivy reminded her.

"Just the once and purely as a political protest."

I pinched the bridge of my nose. "Girls, maybe we could not terrify the traumatized survivors?"

"Sorry," they chorused, not sounding sorry at all.

Joey chose that moment to wake up, blinking sleepily at his audience and making happy gurgling noises. The girls immediately crowded closer, cooing.

"This is Joey," the father said proudly. "I'm Ryan."

I smiled, trying to project warmth and sanity. "It's really nice to meet you—all three of you." I turned to include Hector in my welcome. "I'm Jane." I turned and pointed at the remaining two girls to complete the introductions. "And this is Frances and Ivy."

"Is Joey hungry?" Frances asked. "Does he like ramen? We have lots of ramen."

"And expired crackers," Ivy added helpfully.

"And cream of mushroom soup," Hillary chimed in.

Ryan looked slightly overwhelmed, but was starting to relax his death grip on the happy baby. "He'll eat pretty much anything that isn't moving."

"Perfect!" Taylor squealed.

"Most of our food stopped moving days ago," I assured him. "Except Mr. Vásquez' chickens. But we're not at that point yet."

"Right." Ryan glanced at Hector, who shrugged.

"I have coffee, if you'd like to come in and tell us what you've seen," I offered. "It's only instant, but it's hot and caffeinated, which counts for a lot these days."

The girls had already surrounded Ryan and were gently herding him and Joey toward my house, chattering excitedly. Zeus bounded after them, tail wagging.

I hung back with the other two men. Mr. Vásquez still had an arm around his son's shoulders and a huge smile on his face. I narrowed my eyes at him when he met my gaze and the smile got even wider.

"Your daughters seem nice," Hector commented as we followed at a more reasonable pace.

"They're feral," I told him. "But only two of them are mine. Taylor and Ivy are strays who wandered in from town."

Ahead of us, the girls were showing Ryan their glittery "NO GRMPIES" sign attached to our gate. He looked mildly confused.

"They are very resourceful," Mr. Vásquez said diplomatically.

"Is your husband...?" Hector trailed off delicately.

"Last I heard, my ex-husband was in Paris with his mistress," I said shortly. "I assume this thing has spread worldwide?"

He nodded. "Yeah, that was what they were saying before everything went dark. Cities are the hardest hit overseas, just like here."

We followed the girls into the house and I returned my bat to its position by the door and settled the men around my kitchen table. Ryan reluctantly surrendered his son to the horde of cooing girls and soon the sounds of giggles and baby talk drifted in from the living room.

Frances brought me the kettle and in a minute I was setting four mugs of fresh coffee on the table. Frances leaned a hip against the kitchen counter with an unusually serious expression.

"Don't you want to play with the baby?" I asked hopefully as I sank into my chair.

She ignored me. "How bad is it?" she asked, looking directly at Hector.

His expression darkened. "Bad. The infection spread faster than anyone expected. And then the sick people started getting violent. We weren't prepared. No one was prepared. They called in the National Guard, but..." He shook his head.

"So, no help is coming," I concluded.

"Not anytime soon," he confirmed. "We're on our own for now."

"Speaking of good news," I started and glanced at Luis. "Clyde is driving around playing loud music to attract the infected so he can use them for target practice."

Luis cursed in Spanish. "That *idiota* is going to get us all killed."

"He's treating it like some kind of game," Frances added. "He almost ran Mom and Zeus off the road earlier."

"We'll need to deal with him," Hector said grimly. "Before he draws more attention to the area."

"He tried to get Mom to sell him part of our land," Frances informed them. "He was super creepy about it."

I shot her a look but she just shrugged and said, "What?"

"Do you listen to all of my conversations?" I asked pointedly.

"Pretty much, yeah." Frances waved a hand dismissively.

"Clyde has always been..." Luis paused, searching for the right word. "Difficult."

"That's diplomatic," I muttered.

"But now he is dangerous," Luis finished. "We should warn the others. The Browns, the Hortons, Bobby and his friends—"

"Sarah and Tom are the Hortons?" I interjected.

Luis nodded.

"Is Bobby the tall skinny guy at the drug house? I stopped by to check on them but didn't get a name."

"The drug house? Is that what we're calling it?" Hector lifted an eyebrow, glancing at his father for confirmation.

Luis nodded. "Yes, Bobby and his friends do quite a lot of business."

"Dad!" Hector rebuked him, but Luis waved him off.

"They don't hurt anyone." Luis turned to me. "Hector is a police officer in the city."

"Oh," I replied. That was good to know. "Well, they were getting low on supplies and talking about making a run into town."

Hector straightened. "That's suicide. The town is over-run."

"I told them that," I sighed. "But they all looked strung out and desperate."

"We all need supplies," Frances pointed out pragmatically. "We can't live on ramen and mushroom soup forever."

I sighed again. There was no point in beating around the bush. "They were going into withdrawal, honey."

Frances' eyes widened as realization dawned. "Oh," she said quietly.

"Even if they found what they needed, it would not last forever. It was foolish of them to risk going into the town," Luis said firmly. "We have plenty of eggs, vegetables and fruit, and clean water from the wells," he pointed out. "We are safer here than anywhere else."

A burst of automatic gunfire in the distance punctuated his words.

"With one exception," I muttered.

18

Friday, October 11th

"According to the survey I paid for, this is my property line," I said, gesturing at the wide drainage ditch that ran along the western edge of my land. The stone retaining wall rose about five feet on our side, dropping sharply to create a natural barrier.

"Though Clyde seems to think differently," I grumbled.

Luis made a dismissive noise. "Clyde has been trying to claim both sides of that ditch for twenty years. He used to harass old Bob Peterson about it constantly."

"The previous owner?" I asked, peering down into the ditch. Someone had spray painted what appeared to be anatomically unlikely body parts on the stones.

"*Sí*. He tried to force Peterson to buy the land from him." Luis shook his head. "As if anyone would want that useless strip."

"Clearly you've never seen the artistic additions," I muttered.

Beside me Hector snorted.

The distant rumble of a badly tuned engine was getting closer. Clyde's massive truck appeared at the bottom of the ditch, music blasting.

"Oh good," I sighed. "The floor show is starting."

We watched from the back porch as Clyde drove slowly up the ditch, occasionally stopping to take pot shots at the shambling figures that followed in his wake.

"This is like the world's worst parade," Frances observed. "He's literally hunting zombies while blasting Christian rock." Frances wrinkled her nose. "That's, like, peak Florida Man behavior."

"We're in Virginia," I reminded her.

"Same difference," Frances countered.

I couldn't really argue.

A voice yelled "Mom!" from the depths of the house and Zeus started barking. He ran back inside, the rest of us hot on his heels.

Hillary looked up from her spot on the floor as we entered the living room. "Someone's at the door," she announced, Joey bouncing in her lap.

Taylor and Ivy were on either side of her and Ryan was asleep on the couch.

"Stay," I told her, holding out a hand.

My child barked at me, which I ignored.

I opened the front door to see a thin woman with stringy red hair standing on my porch, arms wrapped tightly around herself. I recognized her immediately.

"It's the girl—Lucy," I told the others, "from the drug—um, from the house down the road."

I opened the storm door carefully. Lucy looked fragile, but much more alert. She was still pale and there were dark circles under her eyes, but they were clear.

"Hi," she said softly. "I'm so sorry to bother you, but. .." She swallowed hard. "Bobby and the others went into town yesterday. Or maybe the day before? I'm not really sure. But they haven't come back and I—" She broke off, tears welling in her eyes.

"Come in," I said gently, stepping back. "When's the last time you ate?"

She shook her head. "I don't know. What day is it?"

"Friday," Frances supplied. "I think."

Lucy laughed, a harsh sound with no humor in it. "I still don't know. I think I've been out of it for a while. What's the date?"

We all stared at her.

"It's Friday, October 11th," Taylor said carefully. "Are you okay?"

"No," Lucy admitted after a long pause. "I haven't been okay in a long time."

I guided her to the kitchen table while Frances started making tea. Luis sat at the table with us, but Hector remained standing. Hillary followed us in, Joey cradled in her arms, trailing Taylor and Ivy.

"I'm in med school," Lucy said suddenly. "In Charlottesville. I went to this party to blow off some steam after finals and..." She accepted the mug Frances handed her with trembling hands. "I just never left."

"Was one of the guys your boyfriend?" Frances asked hesitantly, sitting down at the table.

Lucy's laugh was hollow. "Kind of? I don't really remember. They kept me pretty out of it most of the time."

The implications of that statement hung heavy in the air. I saw the moment Frances figured it out. Her eyes went wide and then hard. Taylor wrapped a protective arm around Ivy, who still looked confused.

"Hills," I said quietly. "Why don't you and the girls go upstairs and try to dig out some of your old baby clothes for Joey?"

For once, Hillary didn't argue. She herded the other girls toward the living room, though Frances shot me a look that clearly said we'd be discussing this later.

"You're safe here," I told Lucy once the girls were gone.

She nodded, tears sliding down her face. "I think it's been four or five days since I've had anything. Everything hurts but I can think again." Her voice broke.

"If Bobby isn't dead," Hector said from behind his father, "he's going to wish that he was."

***

It took several hours and a crowbar to pry Joey from Hillary's cold, dead hands. Actually, the hands were somewhat warm and clammy and there may have been a few tears. Ryan would probably need therapy.

Honestly, we all did at this point. If any therapists survived the apocalypse, they were going to be pretty busy.

The sun was setting as I left the girls crying on the floor of the living room and walked the guys down to our gate. I girded my loins and started perhaps the most awkward conversation of my life.

"So, you're a cop," I said, not looking in Hector's direction.

"I am," he confirmed.

"Have you met Sarah and Tom, in the mobile home about halfway down the mountain?" There was definitely a better way to go about this, but I couldn't think of it.

Hector slowed, his father and Ryan starting down the road to Mr. Vásquez' house. "Yes, I've met them a couple of times. They seem like a nice couple." He put a hand on my arm, drawing me to a stop at my gate. "I saw their car is still in their driveway. Are they okay?"

"No," I said baldly, my gaze locked in somewhere around his collarbone. "No, they aren't."

This was a really inappropriate time to fixate on the tan, warm skin peeking out of the v-neck of this guy's shirt.

"Zeus is their dog, isn't he?" Hector realized. "I've only seen him once, but he's pretty memorable."

"I went to check on them..." I let my voice trail off, trying to piece together the last few days. "Tuesday, I think?"

When I paused again, Hector nudged me gently. "And?"

I met his gaze.

"And Zeus was locked in a bathroom," I continued, without thought.

This was a lot of eye contact. Even though I'd only been divorced for a few months, it had been almost a year since I'd shared a bed with my ex. That must be what was wrong with me. This was not the time for those thoughts.

"There was blood everywhere," I rushed out, to distract myself.

"Damn," Hector sighed, his cheekbones sharp in the evening shadows. "I'm sorry you had to see that—"

"Then Tom came here," I interrupted him, needing to just get it all out. "Well, not here. There. He showed up at my house." I threw my hand in that general direction, finally letting my eyes meet his. "I was working on the fence, with a hammer. And suddenly he was standing behind me. His eyes were red and he tried to grab me and I hit him." I took a deep breath. "With the hammer," I clarified.

Hector didn't seem surprised or shocked or anything really. I guess he's seen a lot more zombies than I have.

"He's dead?" was all that he asked.

I nodded, a lump in my throat. "Completely dead," I clarified, still holding his warm, bottomless gaze.

Hector reached out and touched my hand. "I'm so sorry. It'll be okay."

"Are you saying that as a cop?" I choked out, my voice already wet with unshed tears. "Because I'm pretty sure killing your neighbors is a pretty big issue."

"I'm not a cop right now," he said. "I'm a survivor, just like you." His eyes were a deep velvety brown that burned. "And you did what you had to do."

There was a moment of profound silence, then I blurted out, "His body is behind the garden shed."

19

Saturday

"I really miss the hot water heater," I muttered, hauling another pot of warm water up the stairs. "Actually, I really miss electricity in general. This is getting ridiculous."

Lucy sat perched on the closed toilet lid, looking small and fragile in one of my old college sweatshirts. We'd all been washing up in the sink since the power went out, but her red hair was tangled and greasy, hanging in clumps around her face.

"You don't have to do this," she said softly.

"I know." I set the pot on the floor next to the tub. "But nothing makes you feel more human than clean hair."

She managed a weak smile. "I haven't felt human in a while."

I tested the water temperature. "Well, it's time to fix that. Ready?"

She nodded and leaned over the tub. As I poured warm water over her head, the neckline of the borrowed sweatshirt slipped to one side, exposing the fine bones of her shoulder. Even before the apocalypse, this girl had been starving to death.

"So," I said conversationally as I worked shampoo through her hair, "med school?"

"Second year," she confirmed, voice muffled. "I was going to be a pediatrician."

"Was?"

"Well, it's the end of the world, so it seems unlikely."

I considered this as I rinsed her hair. "I don't know. Seems like doctors might be in pretty high demand these days. Especially ones who can handle both zombies and children." I paused. "Though the difference is probably minimal."

That earned me a real laugh, though it had a slightly hysterical edge.

"My dad would have loved that joke," she said after a moment. "He had a terrible sense of humor."

"Had?" I asked gently, nudging her forward to rinse the suds from her hair.

"He and my mom died in a car accident last year." Her voice was carefully neutral.

I said, "I'm sorry," which felt inadequate.

"Yeah, me too." She was quiet while I worked conditioner through her tangles. "They were amazing parents. Maybe a little overprotective, but they wanted me to have every opportunity. Dad was a professor and Mom was a librarian. They encouraged me to focus on school and not worry about anything else."

"They sound really nice," I said softly.

"They were. It was a good life. Until it wasn't." She sighed. "I kind of lost it when they died. I made it through the end of the semester, but I couldn't handle being at home alone, so I stayed in town after finals. I didn't really have anywhere else to go."

I hummed acknowledgement, carefully working through another tangle.

"Bobby seemed so nice at first," she continued quietly. "One of my roommates invited me to a party at his house." She laughed bitterly. "I'd never even had a beer before that night."

"What did they give you?" I asked, trying to keep my voice neutral.

"I don't know. Everyone was drinking and I didn't want to seem like a prude. By the time he offered me a pill, I was already floating. Then..." She trailed off. "I don't remember much after that. Just fragments. Bits and pieces."

I rinsed her hair one final time, giving her a moment to collect herself.

"I can't believe it's October," she said as I helped her sit up. "I had a 4.0 GPA. I was going to help people, save lives." Her voice cracked. "And then I just slept through the start of the semester. Probably lost my spot in the program. All because I was stupid enough to take a drink from a stranger."

"Hey." I wrapped a towel around her narrow shoulders, giving them a squeeze. Intellectually, I knew she was older than she looked, but under my arm she felt small and fragile.

"That wasn't your fault," I said. "Those guys took advantage of you."

"I should have known better."

"That doesn't make what they did okay," I said firmly.

Lucy stood and stared at her reflection in the mirror, touching her clean hair tentatively. "I look terrible."

"It's the apocalypse. We all look terrible." I caught her gaze in the mirror. "You look like a survivor," I stated. "And that's freaking awesome."

"Thanks," she said softly. "For everything."

"You're very welcome." I squeezed her shoulder. "And for what it's worth, I think you're still going to save lives. Maybe not exactly the way you planned, but the world needs smart people who care about others now more than ever."

She turned to face me, tears in her eyes. "Even if those smart people are recovering addicts?"

"It's the apocalypse," I repeated with a wide smile. "We're all recovering from something."

I pulled her into a hug and she cried into my shoulder for a while. Sometimes you just needed to fall apart before you could put yourself back together again.

When she finally pulled back, wiping her eyes, I said, "Now, let's go downstairs and get you some food. I hope you like Cream of Mushroom soup."

20
Sunday

It was way too early for this shit.

I groaned and buried my face in my pillow, but the gunfire continued, punctuating twanging country music played at stadium levels.

"This is what hell sounds like," I muttered into my pillow.

Zeus whined from his spot at the foot of my bed, clearly sharing my opinion of our neighbor's early morning activities.

I dragged myself to the window just in time to see Clyde take aim at something in the drainage ditch. He was perched on top of the retaining wall like some kind of deranged garden gnome with a rifle.

"Mom!" Frances called from downstairs. "Clyde's doing his thing again!"

"I can hear," I yelled back. "The dead can hear. The undead can hear."

I threw on my slippers and stumbled downstairs to find the girls clustered around the kitchen window, watching Clyde's performance with various levels of horror and fascination.

"Doesn't he know those were people?" Ivy asked quietly.

Lucy, who was looking considerably better after a couple days of actual food and rest, wrapped her arms around herself and shuddered. "I don't think he cares."

"He's treating it like a video game," Frances observed. "Except with real live targets."

"And worse music," Taylor added.

Hillary pressed her face against the glass. "He's reloading!"

"Step away from the window," I ordered. "I don't want any of you getting hit by a stray bullet because Rambo out there can't aim."

"His aim is actually pretty good," Hillary pointed out helpfully.

"Someone needs to talk to him," Frances said, moving away from the back window. "Before he attracts more of them than he can handle."

"I volunteer Mom," Hillary announced.

"Thanks, sweetie."

"You're welcome!" She beamed at me. "Maybe take Hector with you. He's a cop."

"*Was* a cop," I corrected automatically. "And what makes you think Hector would help?"

All five girls gave me identical knowing looks.

"What?" I demanded.

"Nothing," Frances said innocently, nodding her head toward the front windows. "But he's coming up the driveway now and you're still in your pajamas."

I looked down at my ancient SpongeBob sleep pants and threadbare t-shirt. "Crap."

"And no bra," Hillary gasped in mock horror.

"I hate all of you," I informed them, running for the stairs.

By the time I made it back downstairs in actual clothes, Hector was in my kitchen drinking coffee while the girls peppered him with questions about zombies.

"Morning," he said, trying not to smile at whatever my hair was doing.

I grunted in response and grabbed the hot kettle to make my own coffee. Behind me, the sound of gunfire was fading into the distance.

"So," I said, turning to face Hector. "About our neighbor..."

"I can talk to him," Hector offered. "But I don't have any real authority and he knows it."

"Yeah," I sighed, "but someone has to do something before he gets us all killed."

"Are we one hundred percent sure that what he's doing is a problem?" Hillary asked matter-of-factly.

I turned to her, shocked. "What do you mean?"

"He's not shooting people at a Walmart," Hillary pointed out. "He's only killing zombies who are on his property." She pinned me with a stare. "Just like you did."

"That was different," I protested. "Tom was attacking me!"

"So it's okay to kill zombies in self defense but not for fun?" Hillary asked.

"Yes, you psychopath!" I threw my hands up. "How is this even a question?"

"Ethics are complicated in the apocalypse," Frances said calmly.

I pointed my coffee cup at her. "Don't you start."

"I was thinking about checking on the Browns at the bottom of the road," Hector interrupted before the conversation could devolve further. "Want to come?"

"Yes!" I said, probably too quickly. "Get me away from these heathen children."

I set my cup in the sink and grabbed a jacket from the hook by the door.

"Stay in the house," I told the girls. "Zeus is in charge."

The motorcycle was sitting in front of his father's house. It was black and muscular, the cover over the engine polished to a high gloss.

"This is a really nice bike," I observed nervously. I hadn't been on the back of a bike since college.

Hector swung his leg over the seat and gave me a lopsided smile. "I stole it," he admitted, extending his hand.

I slipped my fingers across his warm, calloused palm, and awkwardly hoisted myself onto the seat behind him. And just like that my crotch was resting against his ass. *Oh, my.* I pushed myself back against the seat, only to slide forward again. Hector was very warm and solid and smelled amazing considering we were living through the apocalypse.

Mildly desperate, I tried to scoot back again, squeezing my thighs against his hips to keep myself in place. Ignoring my thrashing behind him, Hector started the bike and we began rolling down the hill. He hit the first pothole and we were plastered against each other again.

I gave up and enjoyed the ride.

At the bottom of the mountain, the Browns' property looked unchanged, except for the addition of some creative anti-zombie defenses involving wind chimes and reflective garden ornaments.

"It's like a fortress designed by Pinterest," I commented as we pulled up to the gate.

Hector laughed, the sound vibrating through my chest where I was pressed against his back. It took a concentrated effort on my part to peel myself off of him and climb down from the bike on unsteady legs.

Mrs. Brown met us at the gate, wielding a cricket bat. "Oh, hello, dears!" she exclaimed in a cheerful British accent. "Hector! It's so good to see you again. I'm sure your father is so relieved." She lowered her weapon and let it swing down by her side. "Quite a spot of trouble we've had lately, isn't it?"

"Just a bit," Hector smiled his agreement. "Have you met Jane?"

The older woman held out her free hand and I grasped it. "Just in passing. It's lovely to meet you, dear. I'm Eileen Brown. My husband James is just having a bit of a nap at the moment. He's a touch under the weather today, or I'm sure he'd be thrilled to meet you."

She ushered us through the gate and two inquisitive goats trotted over to say hi. "Come and sit in the garden and I'll make us some tea," Eileen insisted. "I'm dying to hear any news."

We were settled onto wrought iron chairs and given tea in delicate china cups while Eileen explained their plans for long-term sustainable living through their large vegetable garden and small goat herd.

"The infected don't seem interested in the animals," she told us. "And goats are very practical. Milk, even meat if necessary..." She let the words trail off, her smile fading. "Though we're hoping it won't come to that," Eileen continued. "They're such dear creatures."

We left an hour later with a generous bag of veggies and two jars of goat milk.

"So," I said, carefully cradling the glass jars between us as we pulled away from the Browns' gate. "She's surprisingly resilient."

Hector nodded over his shoulder. "Seriously. Who knew?"

The girls were all thrilled with our haul, especially Lucy. The young woman practically burst into tears as she cradled the jars.

"It doesn't taste great," I cautioned her. "But Mrs. Brown said you can turn it into any kind of dairy product. Like cheese."

"Cheese," Lucy whispered reverently.

Hillary came up beside her, rubbing the outside of the jar in awe.

I ignored them and continued. "They make more milk than they can use and have no way of keeping it cold, so she said we were welcome to come down for more anytime. She's made butter and yogurt out of it, too. Think we can figure it out?"

"Oh yes, definitely." Lucy's smile was slightly maniacal. She turned to Hillary, who wore the same expression.

"Cheeeeese," they whispered at each other, then ran from the room.

"Well," I said, "that wasn't creepy at all."

21

Monday, Maybe

Taylor

Taylor stared at the massive dresser blocking the doorway and wondered, not for the first time, if the apocalypse was just an elaborate cosmic joke. "I don't think it's going to fit."

"It has to," Frances insisted. "It came in this way."

"Did it, though?" Taylor arched a single brow, something she'd spent hours perfecting in the bathroom mirror. "Did you actually see it or is that just what you were told?"

Frances rolled her eyes, unimpressed with the logic nor the eyebrow. "Are you helping move furniture or questioning reality?"

"I'm capable of multitasking." Taylor ran a hand through her hair, grimacing at the tangles. Apparently the end of civilization meant the end of decent conditioner.

"We could take the door off the hinges?"

"I don't think that's going to help."

Taylor considered the problem. "We could set it on fire and claim it was an accident?"

"No arson," Jane called from downstairs.

"She has freakishly good hearing," Taylor muttered.

Frances nodded. "And paranoia."

The Kovak's farmhouse was a little run down but pretty nice. The three bedrooms up here had probably been perfect before the world went to hell and they'd acquired three additional girls and one very large dog. Now, things were getting cramped and some reorganization had become necessary.

"Okay," Taylor said, leaning back against the dresser. "So Hillary and Ivy are sharing the small room at the end of the hall..."

"With the princess curtains and unicorn lamp," Frances confirmed.

"Your mom has the master bedroom..." she continued.

"With the en suite bathroom that we're all totally not jealous of," Frances interjected helpfully.

"Lucy's in your mom's office downstairs..."

"No internet, no work, no need for an office. Her computer is pretty much a fancy paperweight these days."

Taylor frowned at her. "And we need to move this dresser out of this room because...?"

Frances waved her arms. "Aesthetics!"

"Right." Taylor nodded sagely. "Of course. How could I forget about the aesthetics of our post-apocalyptic teenage bedroom?"

"We need the floor space more than the storage," Frances said in a more serious tone. "It's not like you came with a bunch of stuff."

"True." Taylor shrugged and resumed pushing.

From downstairs, they heard Hillary shouting something about cheese and experimental kitchen science.

"Should we be worried about that?" Taylor asked.

"Probably," Frances shrugged. "But I'm choosing to focus on this dresser crisis instead."

They stood in contemplative silence for a moment, studying the furniture blockade.

"We could push it out the window," Taylor suggested.

"No property damage!" Jane yelled up the stairs.

"How does she do that?" Taylor whispered.

"It's a mom thing," Frances whispered back. "Goes along with the eyes in the back of her head."

"That's terrifying."

"I know, right?"

Zeus chose that moment to lumber up the stairs. He stood in the doorway and whined until the girls pushed the dresser back into place against the wall. As soon as the doorway was clear, he slipped into the room, his massive head swinging between them as if checking for treats.

"Hey, buddy." Taylor scratched behind his ears. "Want to help us move furniture?"

Zeus flopped onto his side, effectively claiming the little floor space available in their room.

"I'll take that as a no."

Frances slid down the wall to sit next to the dog. "Maybe we should just leave it here. Turn it into modern art. Call it 'Suburban Decay' or something pretentious."

"Very postmodern," Taylor agreed, joining them on the floor. "We could write a manifesto about how it represents the collapse of society."

"My mom would kill us."

"Yeah, probably."

They sat in comfortable silence, interrupted only by Zeus's occasional snore or fart.

"Do you miss them?" Frances asked suddenly. "Your parents?"

Taylor stared at the ceiling, counting water stains. "Yeah." She swallowed hard. "It's hard not knowing for sure. I mean, I know they're probably gone, but..."

Frances reached over and squeezed her hand.

"Sometimes I feel guilty," Taylor continued. "For leaving them. Is that weird?"

"No," Frances said firmly. "And weird is relative these days, anyway. I mean, Hillary and Lucy are downstairs trying to make artisanal cheese during the zombie apocalypse."

"True."

"I'm glad you're here," Frances said quietly after a moment. "Even if it's because of horrible circumstances."

"Thanks." Taylor managed a small smile. "I'm glad I'm here too. Your mom is pretty cool."

"Don't let her hear you say that. It'll go straight to her head."

"Too late!" Jane called from somewhere below.

"Seriously, how does she do that?" Taylor demanded.

Frances just shrugged.

From downstairs came the sound of breaking glass followed by Hillary's voice: "Nobody panic! The kitchen is only slightly on fire!"

"That's our cue," Frances sighed, standing up.

They carefully climbed over Zeus, who didn't move, and headed downstairs to deal with whatever kitchen disaster was unfolding.

"You know," Taylor said as they descended, "in horror movies, the teenagers always make terrible decisions and split up and die horribly."

"Your point?"

"We're actually doing pretty well, all things considered. We stuck together, found responsible adults, secured shelter..."

"Don't jinx it," Frances warned.

"I'm just saying, we're clearly the smart teenagers in this scenario."

They entered the kitchen to find Hillary and Ivy covered in what appeared to be exploded milk products while Lucy dusted baking soda over a suspicious dark spot on the countertop.

"You were saying?" Frances raised an eyebrow.

"Well," Taylor amended, "some of us."

Jane appeared with a fire extinguisher, looking remarkably calm as she surveyed the chaos. "So," she said conversationally, "how's the furniture rearranging going?"

"Great," Frances lied. "Very productive. Lots of progress."

"The dresser couldn't get through the doorway, could it?"

"It's a metaphor for the futility of human endeavor," Taylor explained.

Jane just stared at them.

"We'll figure it out," Frances promised.

"Uh huh." Jane didn't look convinced but let it slide. "And what exactly happened in here?" She set the unneeded fire extinguisher on the countertop and poked at the charred spot.

"Science!" Hillary declared proudly.

Jane pinched the bridge of her nose. "I don't suppose anyone wants to explain why there are scorch marks on my countertop?"

Hillary, Ivy, and Lucy immediately began talking over each other, each offering a different version of events. Zeus chose that moment to come downstairs, took one look at the kitchen, and retreated to the living room.

"Smart dog," Taylor muttered.

Jane held up a hand for silence. "New rule: no unsupervised kitchen experiments."

"But Mom..." Hillary started.

"No buts. I don't care if you're trying to cure cancer or create the perfect grilled cheese. All future scientific endeavors require adult supervision."

"Technically, I'm an adult," Lucy pointed out.

Jane looked pointedly at the burnt spot. "Are you, though?"

Lucy was smart enough to keep her mouth shut.

"Now," Jane continued, "who wants to help clean this up?"

Taylor and Frances exchanged glances and began backing toward the stairs.

"Nobody move," Jane ordered. "Everyone helps or nobody gets dinner."

"Harsh," Taylor whispered to Frances.

"Strategic," Frances whispered back with a wink.

22

Tuesday

The morning was crisp and clear, which seemed inappropriate for burying the guy you'd bashed in the head with a hammer. In movies, funerals always happen in the rain. But apparently the weather hadn't gotten the apocalyptic memo.

I was waiting by the garden shed when Hector arrived, looking unfairly attractive for someone about to help me move a body. He'd brought a wheelbarrow, which was both practical and deeply disturbing.

"Good morning," he said quietly.

"Is it, though?" I gestured vaguely at the shed. "Tom's behind there. I covered him with a tarp but..." I trailed off, not sure how to finish that sentence.

Hector squeezed my shoulder. "We'll take care of it."

The "it" in question was wrapped in the blue tarp that had once protected my patio furniture. Now it was protecting my sensibilities from the sight of my dead neighbor. The universe had a sick sense of humor sometimes.

Moving Tom was exactly as awful as I had imagined it would be. We managed to get him into the wheelbarrow with a minimum amount of trauma—to us, Tom was past caring—but the whole thing felt surreal.

"I keep wanting to apologize to him," I admitted as we walked toward the spot Luis had suggested for the burial.

"You did what you had to do," Hector said, not for the first time.

"I know. But—" I swallowed hard. "He was an actual person. And now I'm carting his body around like compost."

"Jane." Hector stopped walking, forcing me to stop too. "This isn't your fault."

"Of course it is. I hit him in the face with a hammer until he stopped moving."

"Because he was attacking you." Hector's eyes were intense. "You protected yourself. And the girls, too."

I nodded, not trusting myself to speak.

Luis appeared then, carrying two shovels. I hadn't even thought about how we were going to dig the hole. My planning had stopped at "move body."

"The ground is soft here," Luis said, indicating a spot under an old oak tree. "And it's far enough from the well that it won't cause problems."

I had not considered proper grave-digging etiquette and, although I was grateful that Luis had this knowledge, I really didn't want to know how he'd come by it.

Frances and the other girls emerged from the house, carrying an odd assortment of items. Hillary had wildflowers, probably from the boxes at the front of the house. Lucy had brought a dusty bible that she'd found in a box in the garage. Ivy was clutching a handful of tissues like a lifeline. Ryan followed them with an alert Joey in his arms and Zeus brought up the rear, his big forehead furrowed with concern and confusion.

Lucy stepped forward, her voice timid. "I thought...maybe we could say something? Before?"

I nodded, not trusting my voice.

The actual digging was hard work, but the guys wouldn't let me help. The ground might have been "soft" by Luis's standards, but it was still a lot of dirt to move.

Hector and Luis worked quickly, though. When Luis lowered himself to the grass to take a break, Ryan passed Joey to me and picked up the shovel. The girls and I formed a sort of honor guard around Tom's tarp-wrapped form.

I wasn't sure what constituted "deep enough" for an impromptu zombie funeral, but eventually it looked about right and we lowered the body as carefully as we could. Tom came to rest at the bottom of the hole with a stomach-churning thump, and Lucy stepped forward.

"I don't really remember much from Sunday school," she admitted, flipping through the book. "But everyone deserves something."

"Yea, though I walk through the valley of the shadow of death..." she began, the familiar words falling softly around us. As she reached the end of the prayer and fell silent, Zeus stepped up and laid down beside the hole, his big head resting on his paws.

If lowering the body had been awkward and awful, filling the grave was far worse. Luis and I stood on either side of the hole, taking turns scooping and scattering dirt while the others watched. Each shovelful of dirt felt like an admission of guilt. By the third shovel, I was crying. By the fifth, I could barely see.

Gentle hands lifted the shovel from my fingers and warm arms wrapped around me from behind. Giving in,

I turned to sob into Hector's chest. He smelled like sweat and dirt and something uniquely him. It should have been gross. It wasn't.

"I killed him," I whispered into his shirt. "I killed a person."

"No," he said firmly. "The infection killed him. You just stopped him from hurting anyone else."

I cried harder.

The others continued filling the grave while Hector held me. When it was done, Frances led the girls in gathering stones to mark the spot. They piled them in a rough mound.

"It's not much of a headstone," Frances said apologetically.

"It's perfect," I told her, finally pulling away from Hector's embrace. My face felt hot and my eyes were swollen. I probably looked like I'd been punched in the face by allergies.

Hector kept his arm around my shoulders as we turned toward the house as a group, a weird little family saying goodbye to our neighbor in the strangest way possible. Hillary walked ahead of us holding Joey, her voice drifting back as she sang a made-up song about zombies to the baby as he snorted and giggled.

"Life goes on," Luis said quietly, patting my arm.

"Yeah," I sighed, leaning into Hector's warmth as the others disappeared into the house.

We paused on the back porch.

"It does," he agreed, his gaze soft.

"Thank you," I said quietly.

His arm slid from my back but stopped at my shoulder. "Anytime." Then, after a pause, "Though maybe next time we could do something less depressing. Like chop firewood."

I laughed despite myself. "It's a date."

The words slipped out before I could stop them. Hector's hand on my shoulder gave a brief squeeze, but he didn't comment.

I looked back at Tom's grave one last time and saw Zeus still lying beside it, his head on his paws.

"Zeus?" I called him. "Come on, boy."

The big dog lumbered to his feet and walked to me, leaning his weight against my legs.

I ran my hand over his big, square head with a sigh. "Let's go home, buddy."

Behind us, the sun continued to shine cheerfully on Tom's makeshift grave and the sound of Joey's laughter rang out from the open window. Somewhere in the distance Clyde was shooting at zombies.

23

Wednesday

"That's not how cheese works," I called out, not looking up from the vegetable bed I was thinning. "You can't just add vinegar to goat's milk and expect magic to happen."

"But science!" Hillary protested from the kitchen window.

"Science doesn't override the basic laws of chemistry," I replied, glancing over my shoulder.

Hillary stood framed in the window, her arms crossed over her chest and a pout firmly in place. "How do you know? Have you tried?" she challenged.

I paused, considering. "You know what? You're right." I waved my hand. "Carry on."

"Really?" Hillary sounded suspicious.

I shrugged. "Sure. Go for it." I turned back to my carrots, ignorant to the fates I had just tempted.

"Thanks, Mom! Lucy, get the pressure cooker!"

I looked up sharply. "Wait, we have a pressure cooker?"

The window was empty.

"Hillary?" I called, but I knew I was too late. I considered running after her, but with the electricity out, what's the worst that could happen?

About an hour later, a loud crash from inside the house answered that question.

"Everything is fine!" Lucy yelled.

I sighed and went back to my carrots. The kitchen countertop was already destroyed from their previous efforts. How much worse could it get?

From inside came the distinct sound of something metal hitting the floor, followed by Hillary's voice: "Uh, Mom? What's the melting point of aluminum?"

I closed my eyes and counted to ten.

What the hell was wrong with me? I really needed to stop asking myself these rhetorical questions. When I opened my eyes, the carrots were still there and a quick glance confirmed that there were no flames visible through the kitchen window.

Movement in the drainage ditch caught my eye. One of Clyde's zombies was wandering aimlessly down the hill, bumping along the stone wall. It stopped and looked around, then continued along its way.

There was another crash from inside the house and I sighed, getting to my feet.

"Mom!" Frances appeared at the window. "Hillary and Lucy are trying to make cheese with a pressure cooker from 1908!"

"I'm aware."

"Shouldn't you do something?"

I gestured at my carrots. "I'm gardening."

"The living room is covered in curdled milk!"

"Fine." I stood up, brushing dirt from my knees. "But if we all die of starvation because I didn't thin these carrots, I'm blaming you."

"If we die of starvation it won't be because of carrots," Frances muttered. "It'll be because Hillary and Lucy destroyed all our food trying to make cheese. Or we'll all freeze to death this winter after they burn down the house."

Inside, the damage had migrated from the kitchen to the living room, which looked like a war zone. Zeus was licking milk from the wall and the pressure cooker lay on its side before the fireplace, looking innocuous despite clearly being an instrument of chaos.

"So," I said carefully. "How's the cheese coming along?"

"We're still working out some technical difficulties," Lucy admitted.

"Physics is being uncooperative," Hillary added.

"I see that." I surveyed the damage. "Any casualties?"

"Just our dignity," Taylor supplied from her safe observation point in the doorway.

"And possibly the ceiling," Ivy added, pointing up.

I followed her gesture to find what appeared to be congealed milk products dripping from my living room ceiling.

"That's new," I commented.

"We're trying to create a sustainable food source!" Hillary protested.

"By destroying the ceiling?"

"Scientific progress requires sacrifice," Lucy said solemnly.

"Does it require sacrificing my entire house?"

"Maybe?" Hillary looked hopeful.

I sighed.

As they started cleaning—or at least moving the mess around—I went back to the vegetables. The ditch was blessedly empty of zombies as far as I could see in either direction. After a while, Lucy came outside and sat beside me.

"I'm sorry about the ceiling," she said quietly, playing with the end of her long red braid. "Did you know the proteins in cheese attach to dopamine receptors in your brain?"

She met my gaze.

"I just really want some cheese," she finished softly.

I wrapped an arm around her thin shoulders. "We'll figure it out," I promised. "Maybe without the explosions next time."

Lucy's lips quirked up with a hint of a smile. "At this point, the possibility of cheese is pretty much all I have left to live for."

"That's not true," I said carefully.

"I just—" She gestured helplessly. "It might be. Everything else is gone, you know? My family, my future, med school...but maybe we can have cheese again. It's stupid, I guess."

"It's not stupid," I told her. "But you have more than cheese. You have us."

"A somewhat dysfunctional apocalyptic family," Frances added from behind us, making us both jump as she kneeled down and leaned in against my back.

"With questionable cooking skills," Ivy chimed in, plopping down on Lucy's other side and wrapping the thin girl in a hug.

"And possible structural damage to the living room," Taylor contributed, kneeling behind the two and throwing an arm around each.

Hillary threw herself down to the grass beside our huddle, beaming. "We're basically the Brady Bunch! But with zombies!"

"And better fashion sense," I added.

Lucy laughed through her tears. "You guys are insane."

"Probably," I agreed. "But you're stuck with us now."

"Even if I keep destroying stuff in my desperate pursuit of dairy products?"

"Even then." I squeezed her shoulders. "Though maybe we could try less destructive foods? Like bread?"

"No!" Four voices chorused.

I raised an eyebrow.

"Hillary tried bread yesterday," Frances explained. "It didn't go well."

"It was very dense," Ivy added diplomatically.

"And tasted like cream of mushroom," Taylor said.

Hillary crossed her arms. "It was perfectly good bread," she insisted. "Zeus ate every bite."

I shared a glance with Lucy. "Maybe we should stick to cheese."

24

Thursday

Frances appeared in my doorway at dawn, looking awkward. "Mom?" She shifted from foot to foot. "We have a situation."

I shot up in bed. "Is it the bread thing again? Because I told Hillary—"

"No." She lowered her voice. "We're out of tampons."

I froze. Oh, crap. How had I not thought about this? "Like out-out?"

"Pretty much. Taylor has a couple that she brought with her, but..."

"But we're all going to need them soon," I finished. *Fan-fucking-tastic.* "Okay, I'll figure something out."

Frances nodded and fled, clearly relieved to have dropped this hot potato in my lap.

An hour later I was dressed and full of cream of mushroom soup. I'd searched through every purse, bag, and piece of luggage we owned and turned up a few more, but yeah, this was a problem. Considering and abandoning DIY options, I made a decision and headed down the street with Zeus by my side for moral support.

Hector was out in front of his dad's house, pounding on one of the posts of the fence. Shirtless. With a large mallet of some sort balanced on his bare shoulder.

Oh, my.

I paused for a moment to enjoy the view before clearing my throat. He spun around, mallet raised. A smile stretched across his face when he saw me, throwing his cheekbones into sharp contrast.

"Hey, there," he said, setting the weapon on the ground. "Everything okay?"

He raised one muscular forearm to wipe the glistening beads of sweat from his brow and my ovaries exploded.

"I need a jump," I blurted. Ugh. "I mean, my car needs a jump. Do you think your dad would let me use his truck?"

He straightened up, frowning. "Are you going somewhere?"

"We need supplies from town."

"What kind of supplies? Is someone hurt?" Hector leaned his hammer against the post and reached for the shirt slung over the rail.

"No, nothing like that." I took a deep breath and didn't bother beating around the bush. "We need feminine hygiene products." I made eye contact. "A *lot* of feminine hygiene products."

His expression didn't change. "Tampons?"

"Yes." I was oddly relieved at his matter-of-fact response. "We're out."

"Oh." Wheels were turning behind his eyes. He was catching on fast to the direness of the situation.

"Oh, indeed," I drawled. "This will become an emergency very, very quickly."

He nodded. "I understand."

I squinted at him. "You're taking this very well..."

Hector raised his eyebrows.

"...for a man," I finished.

He smiled and dimples popped out. "I'm a cop," he explained. "I'm not squeamish about bodily fluids."

I nodded. "I guess that makes sense." I waved my arm toward the truck. "So, do you think you can help me get my car running—"

"Jane." His voice was firm. "You're not going alone."

I wanted to argue, but he had a point and although I'd never admit it, I was relieved. The town wasn't safe.

"Fine," I conceded. "But I'm driving."

"No."

"Why not?"

"Because your car won't start," he replied with a grin.

After letting everyone know the plan, Hector and I set off in his dad's truck. He had his service weapon and I had traded Zeus for my trusty baseball bat. We stopped at the Browns' place first, which seemed neighborly. And considering how much goat milk Eileen had given us, I was happy to try to bring anything back for her that she needed.

As Hector stopped his dad's truck in front of their gate, Eileen came bustling out of the house with an entourage of several tiny bleating baby goats.

"Tampons?" Eileen repeated when I explained our mission. "Oh, love, I'm well past all that. But do bring back some tea if you can find any."

"Any particular kind?"

"Anything but dandelion," she exclaimed over the racket of her tiny horned minions. "I've got plenty of that."

"We'll do our best," I promised.

There were a couple of abandoned vehicles along the side of the main road, but otherwise the ride into town was unremarkable.

"It seems so normal," I wondered out loud.

Hector nodded. "Not a lot of people out here, so not a lot of zombies."

I leaned my elbow on the windowsill and stared at the trees flying past. "I picked a really good time to get out of the city," I realized.

Hector glanced over at me, his gaze searching my face. "How did you choose this place? You don't have family here, do you?"

"No," I confirmed. "No family at all, really. I wasn't coming here as much as I was leaving there."

"Not a friendly divorce?" he ventured gently.

I shrugged. "It wasn't horrible, actually." My eyes moved involuntarily to the pale band of skin around my naked ring finger. "I wasn't angry or upset, which I guess is weird. Just kind of disappointed that my ex isn't interested in being a dad anymore, you know?"

Hector nodded. "That sucks. He doesn't want to see the girls at all?"

"Nope." I grimaced. "I get that we're both different people than we were twenty years ago. I can't be mad that we
grew apart. But he just walked away from the life we built
without one conversation."

"He sounds like a dick," Hector interjected with a lopsided smile.

I laughed. "Oh my god, he was. It happened gradually,
over the years. But he turned into such a tool." Our eyes
met and I shook my head. "Literally the kind of person
who is rude to a server and then stiffs them on the tip."

"I can't imagine you married to that kind of guy," Hector
mused out loud.

"Well, good, because I'm not," I said firmly. A thought
struck me and my shoulders fell. "And he's probably dead
now anyway," I said quietly, all my amusement draining
away.

Hector pulled the truck to a stop and I looked up in
surprise to see we were parked outside of the pharmacy.
I'd apparently blathered on about my sad divorce story the
entire ride into town.

Ugh, charming.

I started to open my door and Hector reached across me
to lay his hand across mine.

"Wait," he said softly. His eyes were dark and warm and very close to my face. "Let me take a look and then I'll come back for you, okay?"

"Um, okay," I replied.

Hector leaned back and my brain started functioning again. I wanted to argue, but I'd missed my chance. And he did have an actual gun, so his plan made sense.

My eyes were glued on him as he moved around the outside of the building, carefully checking up and down the block. There were the remains of a car buried into the front of the bakery across the street, the metal frame nothing but a blackened outline. But there were no flames now, and no movement anywhere. The town seemed completely deserted.

The pharmacy itself looked like it had been through a war, which I supposed it had. The large windows in the front were completely broken out and glass glittered across the sidewalk.

"It's all clear," Hector said, returning to the side of the truck. He swung open my door and offered his hand.

I laid my fingers against the rough skin of his palm and jumped down from the truck, letting go as soon as I had both feet on the ground. The glass crunched under my sneakers as I followed Hector into the store.

All things considered, the inside wasn't as bad as it could have been. There'd obviously been some looting, but there was still plenty of stuff on the shelves. I moved quickly to the feminine hygiene aisle, grabbing everything I could find and stuffing it into one of the plastic trash bags I'd brought with me. I hesitated and put a couple of packages back on the shelf. Hopefully there were other survivors wandering around out there who might need these.

Hector appeared at my side, carrying two full bags in one hand and two bottles of bleach in the other. "I'm taking this out to the truck," he said. "Be right back."

I nodded and moved to the far end of the store, looking through the meager grocery offerings. There were lots of fast foods, sodas, coffee...and tea! I grabbed a handful of boxes and threw them into my bag.

I had pulled my list from my pocket when movement from deeper in the store made me freeze.

That was the moment I realized that I'd left my bat in the truck.

25

Still Thursday

Crap. I sucked at this apocalypse stuff.

I backed away slowly, scanning for anything I could use as a weapon. I wasn't sure how much damage I could do with a box of green tea and my charming personality.

A figure rounded the end of the aisle near the dark freezers. Male, probably early thirties, wearing what had once been a nice suit. Now the fabric was torn and dirty and hung off him like he'd lost fifty pounds in the past two weeks.

I tensed, ready to run. But he didn't charge at me like Tom had or make those awful gurgling noises I'd heard from the zombies that had wandered up the ditch. He just stood there, swaying slightly.

Well, this was new.

I mean, I was pretty sure at first glance that he was infected. This guy's eyes were red, just like Tom's had been. The skin around them stained and the whites streaked with lines of blood. But unlike Tom's eyes, his seemed to focus.

On me.

He blinked, then looked up at the ceiling, then at his own hands like he'd never seen them before.

He was definitely infected, but...

"Hi?" I said softly, because apparently I had a death wish.

He leaned toward me, movements jerky but not aggressive. His mouth opened and closed a few times before he managed a rough "Hhhh..."

"Water?" I guessed.

He nodded emphatically.

Oh. My. God.

I glanced toward the front of the store. Where was hell was Hector?

Making another questionable life choice, I grabbed a bottle of sports drink from a nearby shelf.

"This is better than plain water," I said, using my mom voice.

The non-zombie watched as I twisted off the cap, his movements still slow but his eyes tracking.

I moved closer, extending the bottle as far ahead of me as possible. He reached forward and accepted it with trembling hands. I moved a few steps back as he lifted the bottle and drank deeply.

"Th-thankss," he managed after a moment, his voice raw and his words slurred.

"You're welcome." I stayed where I was, maintaining a healthy distance. "How long have you been here?"

His face scrunched in confusion, his head moving back and forth slowly.

Glass crunched near the front of the store and Hector came barrelling down the aisle, gun drawn.

"Jane, get back!" he shouted.

"Wait!" I stepped between them, putting up my hand. "Don't shoot! He's okay!"

"Okay?" Hector questioned, taking in the man's haggard appearance with narrowed eyes.

"Maybe not okay-okay, but—" I struggled to find the words. "Better?"

"Better?" Hector asked incredulously, his gun not wavering.

"He's talking!"

"Zombies don't talk," Hector stated flatly.

"Exactly!" I gestured at our new friend. "But he is. And he hasn't tried to eat me once."

The maybe-former-zombie raised his hands slowly. "N-no eating," he offered helpfully.

Hector's gun didn't waver. "His eyes are red."

"Yes, but his brain seems to be working. Somewhat." I turned back to the man. "What's your name?"

He frowned in concentration. "Mark?"

"Are you asking or telling?" Hector lowered his gun.

The man—Mark?—lurched past me. Hector raised his gun again, but moved to the side as Mark came closer. Mark didn't change direction. He headed toward the front of the store as Hector and I watched, frozen.

"Wait," Hector said, lowering his gun again.

Mark stumbled toward the door with surprising speed for someone who looked like a strong breeze could knock him over.

"Mark!" I called. "We can help—"

But he was already gone.

Hector and I stared at each other.

"That was different," I said finally.

The drive home was quieter, both of us lost in thought.

Finally, I said, "I don't want to tell the girls about Mark. Not yet."

"Why not?" he asked.

"Because hope is dangerous. If I was reading the situation wrong, or it was just a fluke..."

Hector reached across the bench seat and squeezed my hand. "You're not wrong. I saw it too."

I squeezed back, trying not to think about how nice his hand felt in mine. "Still. Let's keep it between us for now."

"And my father."

"And your father," I agreed. "Who, by the way, is a terrible actor. His 'no English' routine was ridiculous."

Hector laughed. "He fooled you for weeks."

"Only because I wasn't paying attention." I paused. "Speaking of paying attention...you can let go of my hand now."

"Do I have to?"

My heart did a completely inappropriate flutter. "Unless you want to crash into Eileen's fence, yes."

He released my hand reluctantly. I tried not to miss the warmth.

After dropping off the tea, we headed back up the mountain. Hector passed his dad's house and pulled right up to my gate, where Hillary was waiting on the porch with her hands on her hips.

"Did you bring me anything?" she demanded.

"Tampons and bleach," I replied cheerfully.

She made a face. "Gross. I meant candy."

"Sorry, fresh out of candy."

"This apocalypse sucks," she declared, slamming back into the house.

26

Friday

Taylor's shriek nearly made me drop the casserole dish of vegan shepherd's pie, which might have been a blessing in disguise.

"I got a signal!" Taylor burst into the kitchen, waving her phone. "Just for a second, but—"

"What kind of signal?" Frances appeared behind her, followed by Lucy and Ivy.

"A bar. On my phone. It's gone now, but—" Taylor's face fell as she stared at her phone. "I swear, it was there."

"Where were you standing?" I asked, trying to stay calm.

"In the backyard. I was taking a picture of Zeus and it just popped up."

"Keep trying," I suggested, setting down the questionable shepherd's pie. "Maybe take something to stand on?"

This led to several minutes of teenagers wandering around holding phones in the air like some kind of post-apocalyptic performance art. Eventually the girls realized they could get a flicker of signal holding their phones out of the upstairs windows. Sadly, an hour later this resulted in me balanced precariously on my roof, holding my phone to the sky.

"This really doesn't seem safe," Hector commented from below.

"Definitely not safe," Luis agreed.

Ryan, holding his son, nodded along and all three men watched with expressions caught between fascination and horror.

"Your concern is noted," I called down. "Taylor, are you sure—" I gasped, "Holy shit, I've got a bar!"

I stared at my phone as if it might explode. Carefully, so carefully, I unlocked the phone without moving its position and tapped on the browser.

"It's spinning!" I announced, excitement coursing through me.

Ten seconds later, "Still spinning."

Two more minutes and, "Still with the spinning," I muttered.

Damn.

"Mom," Frances poked her head out of the window below me. "I don't think it's working."

A gunshot rang out in the distance, making us all jump. I nearly slid off the roof.

Heart pounding, I decided to try again later and began working my way back to the ladder.

"Clyde's at it again," Luis said grimly.

"He's getting worse," Hector added. "Dad saw him setting up speakers yesterday."

"Speakers?" I questioned as I searched for the first rung with my foot.

"On the truck. To make it louder and attract more zombies," he explained. "There aren't as many around anymore, so he's having to work harder to find targets."

I paused on the ladder. "There aren't as many?"

"Yeah. You haven't noticed?" he asked.

Hector steadied the ladder as I descended and I tried not to worry about what view he was getting of my ass.

"I've noticed. We used to get five or six a day wandering up the ditch," Taylor agreed.

Another shot rang out, followed by the distant cackle of Clyde's laughter.

"We should tell them," I whispered softly to Hector as I stepped back onto solid ground.

He didn't ask what I meant. After a moment he nodded.

"Inside, everyone," I yelled. "We need to talk."

We all barely fit in my living room. As we filed in, Francis and Taylor grabbed the couch and Ivy sprawled out on the floor with Hillary and Zeus. Ryan sat in the overstuffed armchair with Joey perched on his lap. Lucy plopped down onto the coffee table, while Hector and Luis stood sentry against the wall, both standing with arms crossed.

Hector nodded his head and I took a deep breath and told them about our encounter with Mark the non-zombie.

The silence that followed was deafening.

"Are you sure he was actually infected?" Frances broke the silence.

I shrugged. "Pretty sure. He had the red eyes, pale face. He looked like all of the others."

"They can get better?" Taylor's voice was barely a whisper.

Frances reached for her hand.

"Maybe," I cautioned. "Frances is right, it's not like I could run a test." I waved a hand toward Hector. "This is why we didn't say anything yesterday as soon as we got home. Even if he was infected and is somehow recovering, it was just one guy. We didn't want to give you false hope."

Lucy was frowning. "Does anyone remember exactly what they said about the virus on the news?" She waved a hand toward the discarded craft supplies still gracing the table she was sitting on. "Hillary said they called it a gram-negative disease?"

"I wasn't paying attention," I admitted.

"They said it wasn't a virus," Hector offered. "My partner was stabbed and the doctor came to tell me he was going into surgery. All of the medical staff were wearing masks, but he said it wasn't a virus." He shrugged. "That's really all I remember."

Ryan nodded. "On the news they kept going back and forth." He patted Joey's back, bouncing his knee as he spoke. "About whether it was bacterial or viral. Whether it was airborne at all." He shook his head, his eyes glistening. "Everyone had a different theory and conflicting advice. Amber wanted to keep Joey home from school on Monday, but she had to go into the office. She wore a mask, but..." His voice broke.

Hector left his position holding up the wall and walked over to lay a hand on Ryan's shoulder. "I'm so sorry," he said softly.

Ryan cleared his throat and continued. "I was working from home. The news was saying that the virus or whatever was affecting the brain, and that's when they started calling it a prion." He shrugged. "Like Mad Cow Disease."

"That can't be right." Lucy leaned forward, resting her elbows on her knees. "Prion diseases aren't airborn. And they permanently alter the brain. It can take years, but it always gets worse, not better. Always."

My mind was spinning. "So if that guy Mark really was recovering, it wasn't a prion disease at all."

"Nope," Lucy confirmed.

"Why does it matter?" Hillary asked from where she sat crossed legged on the floor, petting the dog.

Luis sighed heavily, his arms still crossed over his barrel chest. "Because, *niña,* it means that your grumpies are not really zombies." He glanced at all of us, his face serious. "They are just people who are sick."

"It means they can get better," Taylor choked out.

"And Clyde is shooting them for fun," I added flatly.

27

Friday Afternoon

Motorcycle rides with Hector were becoming my guilty pleasure. My arms wrapped around his trim waist, we bounced down the mountain road under a grey, cloudy sky. The weather was turning cooler and the wind bit through my jacket, giving me an excellent excuse to huddle closer to his warmth.

As usual, Eileen came out to the gate when we pulled up, surrounded by her tiny goat army. Her silver hair was pulled back in a neat bun and she wore a crisp apron over her dress like she was about to film a cooking show.

"Morning, dears!" she called cheerfully, waving as I dismounted with as much grace as I could muster. Which, it turned out, was not a lot. "Ready for more milk?"

"Actually," I said awkwardly as I regained my footing, "we needed to talk to you about something we saw in town."

Her expression changed instantly. "Oh?"

"We probably should have said something yesterday, but we were trying to figure out what it meant before we got everyone excited."

"Excited?" she asked, her face blank.

Hector and I shared a glance.

"We ran into one of the infected in town," Hector began, trailing off.

I took a deep breath, and picked up the verbal baton. "We think the infected may be recovering and we need to figure out how to get Clyde to stop shooting them," I finished in a rush.

Eileen didn't respond for a moment. Then she dusted off her hands and reached out to open her gate. "Let's go inside, dears. It's getting cold out here and I'll make you some of that lovely new tea you brought back for me."

That was unexpected. In all our visits, we'd never been invited into the house.

The tiny goats followed us up the path to the door, bleating encouragement. Or possibly criticism. It was hard to tell with goats. Eileen shooed them away at the door and we stepped inside.

The interior of the cottage was cozy and neat, with cheerful curtains and comfortable furniture. A fire blazed cheerfully in the hearth and a naked man was bound to a bed in the middle of the living room.

I stopped so abruptly that Hector ran into me from behind.

The man appeared to be in his seventies or so, sparse white hair peeking over the padded strap that held his head to the bed. More restraints encircled his wrists and ankles. He had the red eyes of the infected, but he wasn't thrashing or yelling. He just laid there, only his eyes moving as they tracked Eileen's path across the room.

"Meet James, my husband," Eileen said matter-of-factly, as if having your husband tied up naked in the living room was perfectly normal. She bustled around the bed, throwing a clean, white sheet over James' lower half.

She turned back to us with a smile. "Tea?"

"Um," I managed.

"Yes, please," Hector said smoothly, steering me toward the small round kitchen table.

"So others are starting to recover as well," Eileen said, setting a pretty tea tray on the table. "Sugar?"

"Recover?" I squeaked.

"Yes, dear." She poured tea with steady hands. "James started showing symptoms about ten days ago. Tried to bite me, poor love." She glanced over toward the man in question with an affectionate smile. "I had to hit him with the frying pan. He'll be cross about that when he's better, I expect."

James gave no reaction to indicate he understood Eileen's confession, but his eyes never left her.

I accepted a cup of tea automatically, my brain still trying to process what I was seeing. "You've been caring for him by yourself this whole time?"

"In sickness and in health, as they say." She settled into her own chair. "I was a nurse for over forty years, you know."

"But..." I glanced at Hector, who looked as stunned as I felt. "Weren't you afraid?"

"Oh, certainly." She sipped her tea. "But I knew he'd get better."

"You did?" Hector asked.

"Well, not really. At first I just had to believe it because I couldn't accept anything else." She gestured toward James. "His fever broke this morning. Since then he's been much calmer and I've started cutting back on the sedation."

"Sedation?" I parroted dumbly.

"To keep him calm," Eileen explained. "I've been giving him fluids as well, of course."

"Of course," I nodded.

"I've noticed fewer infected walking along the main road the last couple of days." Eileen topped off our cups. "I expect we'll see many more recovered soon. The weather's changing, you know."

"The weather?" I asked. I was definitely not carrying my end of this conversation.

"Everything is worse in summer," she said, as if this were obvious. "Now that it's cooling off, things will settle down."

I exchanged looks with Hector again. "That...actually makes a weird kind of sense."

"Of course it does." Eileen stood and moved to adjust James's IV. "But we need to prepare for winter. Have you started winterizing your houses yet?"

"Um, no?" I admitted.

She clicked her tongue disapprovingly. "You'll want to get on that. It's going to be a while before things are back to normal and we'll have an early frost this year. I can feel it in my bones."

Of course she could.

Thunder rumbled in the distance and Eileen nodded sagely. "Speaking of weather, you'd better head back before the storm hits. Take some milk with you."

We left with two jars of goat milk and approximately eight million questions. The rain started just as my house came into sight, fat drops splattering against the top of my head. I tucked myself against Hector's back, huddling over the milk, but by the time we reached my house, we were both soaked. I climbed off the bike on shaky legs, partly from the cold and partly from processing everything we'd learned.

"So," I trailed off. "That was..."

"Yeah," Hector agreed.

We stood there in the rain, staring at each other.

"They're going to get better," I said slowly.

A smile grew across Hector's face. "Yeah."

"As long as Clyde doesn't kill them all," I cautioned.

His smile faded a little bit. "Yeah, I'll go up there in the morning and talk to him."

I nodded. "And apparently, Mrs. Brown's bones can predict the weather."

Hector laughed, the sound bright against the grey sky. He reached up to brush wet hair from my face. "You're shivering."

"It's raining," I pointed out helpfully. Conversationally, this had not been a good day for me.

"You should go inside."

"Yeah."

Thunder crashed directly overhead, making us both jump.

"Inside," Hector said firmly, dropping his hand.

"Right." I cleared my throat. "Thanks for the ride."

I passed him one of the jars of milk and he tucked it into his jacket, then swung the bike back around. I stood in the rain and watched him drive down the road and into his father's drive before walking into my own house.

28

Saturday

I was no stranger to insomnia, but these days we were BFFs. No matter how many breathing exercises I tried, my brain just wouldn't stop it with the bad news. Like how the man down the road is probably an actual psychopath or we were all going to freeze to death over the winter.

Eileen was right. Even if the non-zombies were recovering, it was going to take a while to get civilization back online. We were going to have to make it through this winter without access to electricity, grocery stores, or the McDonald's drive thru.

Around five, I finally gave up on sleep and threw a couple of layers of clothes on over my PJs and ventured downstairs with Zeus on my heels.

The storm that had drenched me and Hector on the way back up the mountain yesterday afternoon was still going strong, rattling the windows and making the house creak.

I was getting better at building a fire over the last few days, but I still struggled to produce a sad little flame. It waved at me cheerily from the grate, trying its best to dispel the damp from the room.

"Jane Kovak, fire master," I announced to the empty room. "Capable, independent woman—"

The first notes of "The Devil Went Down to Georgia" filtered through the rain, cutting off my self-aggrandizing speech.

"You have got to be kidding me."

I peered outside. It was still mostly dark. Although the rain had slowed to a drizzle, there was zero visibility.

What the actual hell?

"It's not even six!" I yelled at the window. "What kind of psycho goes zombie hunting before breakfast on a Saturday? In the fucking *rain*?"

The kind that lived next door to me, apparently.

I stormed out onto my back porch, Zeus by my side, and sure enough, Clyde was driving up the ditch followed by a horde of the infected like some demented pied piper. I stomped through puddles to the top of the retaining wall, arms akimbo.

"What the hell are you doing?" I screamed over the racing violin chorus and Zeus' barking.

Clyde's truck slowed and he stuck his head out the window, rain dripping off his camouflage baseball cap. "Morning, sugar! Want to join the party?"

"Turn that off!" I gestured wildly at his speakers. "You're going to wake up the whole mountain!"

"That's kind of the point!" He grinned. "Got to get them moving early, before they get too sluggish!"

"Sluggish?"

Behind his truck, about a dozen of the infected stumbled through the couple of inches of water running down the ditch. They moved differently than before. They seemed less aggressive, more confused. Like people waking from a bad dream.

"You've got to stop doing this," I said sharply. "You can't just—"

"Can't just what?" He turned down the music to a dull roar. "Can't protect our community from these monsters? Someone's got to do it!"

"They're recovering!" The words burst out of me.

Hector was supposed to deliver this news with his law enforcement gravitas, but he wasn't here and I had to say something.

So I screamed at the armed man, "They're sick people who might get better if you'd stop shooting at them!"

Lightning cracked overhead. I jumped and Zeus started barking again. Perfect dramatic timing, universe. Thanks for that. I shushed Zeus, pulling him to my side.

"Better?" Clyde's laugh was uglier than the thunder that followed. "That what you think, city girl? That the zombies are going to just get better like in some Hollywood romcom and we'll all be friends again?"

Movement caught my eye at the house. Pale faces were peeking out of my back door, but I waved them back and returned my focus to Clyde. I had to make him understand.

"They're already getting better," I insisted.

"Mom!" Frances called out as the heavens opened and the rain became a solid curtain of water.

Clyde pulled his cap lower and gestured toward the house with his chin. "Go back inside your house, woman, and leave the hard work to the men. This is my mountain to protect."

"You're not protecting anyone," I yelled over the roar of the rain, ice cold water plastering my hair to my face. "You're not the hero. You're just a sad little man who finally found an excuse to murder people without consequences!"

Clyde's face darkened. "Careful what you say to me, sugar. Your eyes are looking a little red this morning. Might have to add you to my collection."

"Mom!" Frances's frantic voice cut through the rain. She was standing on the porch with the others, Taylor clinging to her arm, sobbing.

I turned back to Clyde as another bolt of lightning streaked across the sky. The music abruptly died and smoke began rising from his speakers. I lifted my gaze in thanks to whoever might be up there as Clyde started cursing. He watched, infuriated, as his zombies wandered back down the hill.

Immediate crisis averted, I left him to it and dragged Zeus back to the house, cold and wet all the way through to my underwear.

In my kitchen, Taylor was sobbing in Frances's arms while Ivy hovered nearby looking lost. Lucy appeared with a towel and began drying off Zeus.

She frowned at me. "You need to go change right away," she scolded.

"I will," I waved her away. "Is Taylor okay? What happened?"

A knock at the door made us all jump.

Ivy peeked through the window. "It's Hector!"

I yanked open the door to find him looking as drenched as I was.

"Heard shouting and Clyde's music cut off," he explained, stepping inside. "Everything okay?"

"Just having a neighborly chat," I said dryly.

"We have to stop him," Frances insisted. "Taylor thinks she saw—" She stopped short, looking at the other girl, still holding her hand. "Tell them," Frances urged her.

Tears still streaming, Taylor took in a sobbing breath. "I saw my parents," she blurted, pressing her free hand against her mouth.

Ivy moved to Taylor's other side, running a hand over her back, tears streaming down her own face.

Oh, crap. "In the ditch? Are you sure?" I asked.

Taylor nodded. "I'm so scared," she said. "I want to go after them but I'm afraid they'll hurt me. Or I'll have to hurt them." Taylor looked around the room, desperate for a solution.

Frances drew Taylor into her arms and Ivy sandwiched the sobbing girl between them. Frances met my gaze over her head.

"We can't let that guy shoot them," Frances stated.

"No," I said. "We can't let him shoot anyone else."

"Agreed," Hector said.

I ran my fingers through my wet hair, grimacing at the tangles. "I need to change. Then we need a plan." I pointed at Lucy. "Can you get some breakfast going for the girls? And maybe restart my sad attempt at a fire?"

She nodded, already moving toward the kitchen.

"I'll take care of the fire," Hector volunteered, following her.

I turned to Frances. "Do you know where Hillary is?"

"Asleep? It's still basically the middle of the night."

Upstairs, Hillary was still indeed snoring through the drama and I left her to it. In my room, I peeled off my wet clothes and pulled on dry ones, my mind racing. What I would give for a hot shower right about now. When I came back down, Hector was stoking a proper fire in the fireplace while Lucy and Hillary distributed plates of eggs and hashbrowns. The scene was so domestic it made my heart ache.

"We need to talk to him," Hector said as I approached. "Make him understand."

I snorted. "Because that worked so well just now?"

"No, I mean really talk to him. Show him proof. Take him to see James."

"What if he decides to shoot James instead?"

"We won't let him do that, but if he tries then we'll deal with him accordingly."

I raised my eyebrows. "Deal with him accordingly?" I repeated.

"I'm still a cop," he reminded me quietly. "If he's deliberately killing innocent people, that's murder."

"So now you're a cop again?" I challenged. "Is there even a police force? A government?"

"There's still right and wrong," he said firmly. "Tom's death was self-defense, Jane, but Clyde has crossed a line."

"I know that," I sighed, deflating.

The girls were huddled on the couch. Taylor had stopped crying but she looked haunted. She sat pressed tight against Frances, their hands knotted together.

"Okay," I said finally. "Let's go talk to him. But first..." I grabbed Hector's arm and dragged him into the kitchen. "What exactly does 'deal with him accordingly' mean? Because I think we're going to need a plan B."

Hector ran a hand over his face. "Honestly? I'm just going to shoot him." He shrugged. "It's not like we can hold him for arraignment. But first we'll give him a chance to stop on his own."

"Agreed." I leaned against the counter. "So what's plan A?"

"We go to his house. Try to reason with him. And if that doesn't work..." He waved his hand. "We improvise."

"This feels like a terrible idea."

"You got a better one?"

"No," I admitted. "But I'm pretty sure Clyde is done for the day, so let's wait until it stops raining."

He looked down at his soaked clothes. "Now that's a good idea."

29

Feels like a Tuesday

I t rained for three days and three nights. We stayed in, and didn't hear a peep out of Clyde, so we hoped he was staying in as well. There were also no zombie sightings. Taylor was a bit of a wreck, but it was a much-needed respite for the rest of us. Finally, on what I was pretty sure was the third Tuesday of the apocalypse, the sun finally came out.

Winter was well and truly here and everyone was wearing multiple layers to keep warm, despite the fire that burned constantly in the living room. Lucy had concerns about carbon monoxide poisoning, so we cracked the window. It did kind of seem to defeat the purpose of running the fire, but Lucy was the only one of us with any scientific background, so we humored her.

I had abandoned all of my outdoor projects during the downpour, which gave me the perfect opportunity to finish unpacking the last of our boxes. I'd found some more old baby clothes, a stash of tiny t-shirts and baby legwarmers, and set them aside for Joey.

After breakfast I left the girls playing Uno in the living room and walked the baby clothes down the road. When I knocked on Luis's door Ryan greeted me with a bundled up Joey on his hip. The baby was sporting a long-eared bunny costume from the first bundle we'd given them when they arrived and my heart melted.

"I loved that outfit," I sighed, my long dormant ovaries giving a half-hearted twinge. "Give," I demanded, trading the bag of clothing for the fuzzy baby-bunny.

Joey was such a trooper. He'd gotten quite used to being passed around among the girls and came into my arms with a smile. I breathed in the baby scent and gave into the nostalgia for a long moment.

Surfacing from my baby fever, I found Ryan laying out the clothes on Luis's kitchen table.

"These are wonderful, Jane," he said with a soft smile. "Thank you so much."

"I'm just glad I still had them," I reassured him. "It's been absolutely freezing." The small kitchen was cool. "You guys are doing okay here?"

"We're good," Ryan nodded, but a blush rose across his cheeks. "I may have let the fire burn out," he admitted. "Luis is working on the south field and Hector went to siphon gas from Tom's SUV." Ryan grimaced. "I got distracted feeding Joey."

"Is it going now?" I asked.

"I think so." Ryan ducked his head around the corner to check the living room. "Yup. Looking good now."

"Good!" I shifted Joey in my arms and gave him a kiss on the forehead before handing him back to his father. "I'll see if I can catch up to Hector. I want to ask him about going to check on the Browns again."

Ryan's face became tense. "To see if Mr. Brown has recovered?"

I nodded, my heart breaking for him.

Reaching out, I squeezed his hand where it rested on Joey's back. I couldn't say anything over the lump in my throat, so I slipped out of the door with a wave. Wiping the tears from my eyes, I started walking down the mountain road.

I'd never admit it out loud, but there was a coldly practical part of me that was almost relieved at the possibility of my ex-husband being dead. I wouldn't have wished him dead—for the girls' sake, if nothing else. But now that it was likely, I realized that it would be so much easier to mourn him than to forgive him. Like, if I didn't have to hear about him screwing his secretary in Paris, then the memories of the good times could be bittersweet, not just bitter.

I pulled my jacket tighter around myself, wishing I'd thought to grab a scarf. The sun was bright but offered little warmth, and my breath came out in little puffs of steam.

Hector was exactly where Ryan had said he would be, crouched beside Tom's abandoned SUV with a length of clear tubing in his hand. He looked up at my approach, his face breaking into a warm smile that did more to chase away the chill than the wan sunlight.

"Need a hand?" I asked, knowing full well that he didn't.

"I'm good," he replied, standing and wiping his hands on his jeans. "But I wouldn't mind the company."

Hector had the SUV unlocked and the little door to the gas tank was open. From the back of the big car he produced a funky little spout.

"You found the keys," I exclaimed, my brain playing catch up.

He shook his head with a smirk and nodded toward a long, thin piece of metal leaning against the front of the car. "Nope, I jimmied it open."

"Interesting skill set you have there, officer." I put a hand on my hip and raised one brow.

He laughed. "You'd be surprised how often I've needed to get into locked cars for completely legitimate reasons." Hector inserted the spout into the gas tank, then the hose. "I could hotwire it, too. But the gas will go a lot further in the bike."

"We should check on the Browns before we talk to Clyde," I blurted out.

His expression grew serious. "Yeah. No sense in reenacting the shootout at the OK Corral if we're wrong about the recovery."

"For everyone's sake, I hope we aren't." I frowned. "If Taylor's parents are still alive, maybe other people are, too. Ryan's wife…" I let my voice trail off.

There were a whole lot of people who might still be alive.

"I know." He capped off the gas can and started off toward his father's house. "Ready for another ride on the bike?"

"I think I'm becoming kind of fond of the bike," I admitted.

"Just kind of?" Hector's grin was infectious. "I thought maybe I'd won you over."

"To motorcycles or to you?" Oh, I did *not* mean to say that out loud.

Hector's eyes darkened and the air between us suddenly felt charged. "Both," he said softly.

The ride down the mountain was simultaneously thrilling and terrifying. The road was a mess from the days of constant rain and I clung to Hector's back as he navigated around the worst of the mud and potholes.

As we rounded the last curve before the Browns' property, we saw a tall figure outside, methodically chopping wood. He looked up at the sound of the motorcycle, waving cheerfully.

"Is that James?" I asked in awe when Hector brought the bike to a stop.

"Good morning!" Eileen called, coming out of the house with a tea towel in one hand. "You're just in time for tea."

I practically fell off the bike in my hurry to hug her. She patted my back with her empty hand as I mildly lost my shit.

"There, there," she said soothingly. "I told you he'd get better."

James walked over, axe propped against his shoulder. "Eileen tells me I gave everyone quite a fright," he said in his crisp British accent. "Terribly sorry about that."

"You don't remember?" Hector asked.

James shook his head. "Last thing I recall is feeling feverish. Then nothing until I woke up tied to the bed." He smiled fondly at his wife. "Bit kinky for our age, but I won't be the one to complain."

"James!" Eileen scolded, but she was smiling and her eyes sparkled. "Let's all get inside where it's warm, shall we?"

The older man set his ax by the door and we followed him into the house. Inside, the hospital bed and IV bags were all gone.

Eileen dropped into a chair, her smile softening. "Sit, dears, and I'll tell you what I've learned."

The ride back up the mountain was a blur. My mind was racing a million miles a minute as I considered the implications of James' recovery. Joy for everyone who might get their loved ones back warred with horror at those who wouldn't. There were a lot of people who wouldn't be coming back, and it wasn't because of the infection. It was because of people like Clyde.

People like me.

"Jane?"

Hector's voice pulled me from my thoughts and I raised my head from where I had tucked it against his back. We were sitting on the side of the road, about halfway up the mountain and the air was freezing cold against my face. I raised my hands to wipe away the tears I hadn't realized were falling.

"Hey," Hector said gently, turning on the bike to face me. "What's wrong?"

"Tom," I choked out. "He might have gotten better."

"Don't." Hector pulled me into his arms. "Don't do this to yourself. You didn't have a choice. He was attacking you."

"But if I'd just—I don't know—incapacitated him somehow—"

"How? If you wouldn't have killed him, it's far more likely he would have killed you." Hector's arms tightened around me and his warmth sank into my chilled body. "You did what you had to do in that moment to protect yourself and the girls."

I buried my face in his chest, breathing in leather and motor oil and something uniquely Hector. "I just keep seeing his face."

"I know." His hand stroked my back. "But you're not Clyde. You didn't want to hurt anyone. There's a difference."

I nodded against his chest, trying to believe him.

We stayed like that for a long moment before I finally pulled back, wiping my eyes.

"Sorry," I mumbled. "Didn't mean to fall apart on you."

"Anytime," he said softly, tucking a strand of hair behind my ear. His hand lingered on my cheek and I leaned into his touch.

30
Wednesday

NATIONAL EMERGENCY RESPONSE

I stared blankly at the words in all caps across the top of the screen, not believing my eyes.

"Mom?" Frances called from below. "Did you get any-thing?"

My hands trembled as I took a bunch of screenshots, terrified of losing the message. The single bar at the top of the screen flickered and died, but I had what I needed.

I carefully made my way down the ladder, phone clutched to my chest like a lifeline. When I made it down to Frances, who had been holding the bottom of the ladder, I handed her the phone.

"I got something," I managed, my voice surprisingly steady considering how badly my hands were shaking. "I got something."

Frances took the phone, her eyes growing round. She pressed one hand over her mouth as she read the screen.

"What's going on?" Hillary asked, walking past holding a chicken.

"I got something," I repeated.

"Something?" Hillary looked from me to Frances, who was still frozen, staring at the phone in her hand. "Holy shit!" Hillary yelled. She tossed the chicken into the air and dashed into the house, yelling for the other girls.

The indignant chicken flapped past me and some small part of my mom brain nudged at me to comment on her language. I ignored both of them. If there was ever an expletive-worthy event, this was it.

Lucy burst out of the house, followed quickly by Taylor.

"Hillary said you got something on the phone?" Taylor demanded, panting.

I nodded, still not able to speak.

"It says services are being restored," Frances read in a shaky voice. "It has instructions and links to maps and medical centers and stuff." Frances tapped her finger to the screen and we all waited, but nothing happened.

I looked over her shoulder. "No service down here," I was finally able to say. "I can go back up, but let's read through the main page first. There's a lot. I took screenshots, too, just in case."

Frances nodded and continued reading. "It says 'The viral outbreak is stabilizing across all regions. Reports confirm that infected individuals are beginning to recover. Efforts to provide medical aid and food to survivors are underway.'"

Hillary and Ivy stumbled out of the house as she was reading. Ivy stood in shock, listening, and Hillary bounced on her toes in excitement. Zeus had no idea what was going on, but he barked in solidarity until we all shushed him.

Frances continued, listing general timelines for restoration of electricity and cell service in various regions, where to get medical services, and tips for dealing with people recovering from the infection.

When she finished, Taylor held out her hand and Frances passed her the phone. Her eyes scanned the page, line by line, and tears rolled down her face. Turning, she buried her head in Frances's shoulder, breaking down into sobs.

I rescued the phone from her loosening grip. "I'm going to run down the road and show the guys."

Hector answered the door on the first knock. His eyes widened at whatever he saw on my face. "What's happened? What's wrong?"

Once again at a loss for words, I just handed him the phone. His chocolate brown eyes began to glisten as they scanned the page. "Oh my god," he whispered. "I can't believe it."

"This should make it easier to convince Clyde to stop shooting people," I said. "He doesn't have to take our word for it."

"I'll go with you," Luis spoke up from behind Hector. He and Ryan were sitting at the kitchen table and I hadn't even noticed them. "I've known Clyde for many years. He may listen to me."

"Or he may shoot us all," I offered giddily. The relief flooding through me was completely canceling out my usual cynicism.

"He won't," Luis said with quiet confidence. "He's not evil, just scared and angry. Like we all were."

I caught Hector's eye and nodded. "Okay. Let's go talk to him."

We stopped at the house to let the girls know where we were going and then started up the mountain. The walk to Clyde's property seemed both too long and too short. We moved in silence, my phone heavy in my pocket like a talisman. Luis led the way, with Hector and me following side by side, our shoulders occasionally brushing.

The sound of a rifle being chambered stopped us in our tracks.

"That's far enough," Clyde's voice carried from somewhere above us. "This is private property."

"We need to talk," Luis called back, his hands raised peacefully. "We have news from the government."

Clyde's laugh was harsh. "There ain't no government anymore."

I finally spotted him, perched on a wood deck built about halfway up a large tree. He was standing with his legs spread, some kind of long-barrel rifle pointed in our direction.

"You're wrong." I pulled out my phone, holding it up. "We finally got a signal. The government is getting things under control. The infected are recovering, just like I told you."

"Bullshit."

"It's true." Luis took another step forward. "Remember James, at the bottom of the mountain? He's completely recovered. Come see for yourself."

There was a long pause. "James was infected?"

"And he's fine now," I rushed to point out. "Eileen had him tied to the bed for two weeks with an IV and now he's completely back to normal."

"You know me, Clyde," Luis said softly. "Have I ever lied to you?"

Another pause, longer this time. Finally, Clyde lowered his rifle. "Show me," he demanded.

Luis held his hand out for the phone and I handed it over. He walked to Clyde's tree and climbed up a ladder attached to the trunk. It was uneven and rickety and I held my breath as Luis moved slowly upward. When he reached the bottom of the platform he lifted his arm, phone extended. Clyde snatched it from his hand, squinting at the screen.

"This could be faked," he said, but his voice had lost some of its edge.

"It's real," Hector spoke up. "And you know it. You've seen them changing, getting slower, less aggressive. That's why you've been hunting earlier, trying to get to them before they recover enough to speak."

Clyde's face twisted. "They're dead. You don't come back from dead."

"They're not dead," I insisted. "Zombies aren't real." I swung my arm out toward the road leading down the mountain. "Listen, dead people don't move around. These people aren't dead, they're just sick. And if you keep shooting them, you'll be murdering innocent people who might have families waiting for them to come home."

My words hung in the air. I looked back at Hector, who gave me a small nod.

"No," rang with a finality that echoed through the trees.

Clyde tossed the phone all the way down to the ground, where it landed in the leaves at the base of the tree with a soft thud.

Luis moved quickly down the ladder and dug through the ground cover to find it.

"Get off my land," Clyde said coldly, the barrel of his big gun swinging back up to point in our direction.

And just like that the frozen feeling I'd had since I first saw the one little bar appear on my phone was gone.

"Are you fucking kidding me?" I asked coldly, my voice rising. "I'm warning you right now," I told him, taking a step forward. "You'd better not shoot one more goddamn person, Clyde Johnson."

"Or what?" he sneered down at me from his little nest. "Nothing matters anymore. This is all bullshit." He raised one arm from his rifle to swing it out. "All of this? All of this is *over*. Nothing fucking matters anymore and I'm going to do whatever the hell I want." His hand came back to the gun and he aimed it right at my head. "Now I'm not going to tell you again. Get off my land."

"Where is Bernadette, Clyde?" Luis asked softly.

Clyde froze, the blood running from his face, leaving his skin pale except around his eyes, which looked bruised.

Long moments passed in silence, until I couldn't stand it anymore.

"Who the hell is Bernadette?" I whispered to Hector.

He shrugged, his gaze sliding over to his father. "Dad?"

Luis ignored him, his eyes locked onto Clyde. "Was Bernadette in the city when this all started?" he asked. "Did she come home infected?"

Clyde didn't respond, but his lips pressed together, thinning to nothing. He tucked the end of the rifle against his shoulder and a clod of dirt exploded about five feet in front of us.

I jumped and may have peed a little.

"That was your one warning shot," he said, not a drop of emotion in his voice. "Get out."

31
Still Wednesday

The walk back down the mountain was surreal. Every few steps, I'd touch the phone in my pocket, reassuring myself that it was real—that the message was real. The infected could recover. *Were* recovering. There was a light at the end of this tunnel—and for once it wasn't the god damn train.

"You okay?" Hector asked softly, his shoulder brushing mine.

"Yeah," I replied quietly. "Just processing."

Luis walked ahead of us, muttering under his breath in Spanish.

Hector jogged a few steps to catch up with his father. "What was that about?" he demanded. "Who is Bernadette?"

"Clyde's wife," he said shortly. "I'm guessing she was infected and Clyde put her down."

"Oh, no," I whispered. I understood guilt. My steps slowed and I fell back, my mind racing.

Wait.

"That asshole hit on me!"

When we reached my driveway, Hector touched my arm. "We should get back. Ryan's not great at keeping the fire going."

I put my hand over his. "I'll tell the girls what happened. Do you guys all want to come over for dinner? We have eggs and potatoes and something that's almost cottage cheese."

"That sounds wonderful," Hector agreed.

They headed back down the road and I climbed the steps to my front porch, still feeling slightly untethered from reality. The girls were clustered in the living room, faces expectant.

"Well?" Frances demanded.

I sank into the armchair, not sure how to explain Clyde's reaction. "He didn't take it well."

"What does that mean?" Taylor asked, her voice small.

"We thought we heard a shot," Frances let the statement hang in the air as a question.

I nodded. "He fired a shot into the dirt."

"Did you poop your pants?" Hillary asked, her expression intent.

"Geez. No, I didn't poop my pants." I rolled my eyes at her.

"Did you pee a little?" she asked.

I frowned at her. "That's not important. The important thing is that we need to protect the infected from Clyde until help gets here, and I may have an idea how to do that."

"Hector can just shoot him," Frances muttered.

I shrugged. "That's definitely still an option. But I was thinking we could throw stuff into the ditch to block it. That way he can't lure them up here."

"What kind of stuff?" Lucy asked.

Before I could answer, the distinctive rumble of Clyde's truck echoed up the ditch.

"Is that—" Hillary started.

"Oh god," Taylor gasped.

We all froze for a split second, then burst into motion. I grabbed my baseball bat from the front door and followed the girls through the house.

Taylor got to the back door first, yanking it open and sprinting outside. The rest of us spilled out into the backyard.

A moment later the top of Clyde's truck crested the curve of the ditch. "Sweet Home Alabama" blasted from his speakers at full volume. He must have gone straight home and grabbed his gear after we left.

"No," Taylor cried out from where she stood at the edge of the ditch. "Jane, I see them. I see my mom and dad!"

I pushed past her, running toward the retaining wall.

"Clyde!" I screamed. "Stop!"

He ignored me, continuing up the ditch. Behind his truck, I could see shapes moving in the growing darkness.

"Mom?" Frances called from behind me. "What do we do?"

What *could* we do? I looked around frantically, searching for anything that might help. My eyes landed on the pile of rocks Hillary had been collecting.

"The rocks," I yelled. "Throw the rocks at his truck!"

The girls scrambled to gather stones, pelting the truck with surprisingly good aim, while Zeus barked his head off. One particularly large rock hit Clyde's windshield with a sharp crack. He slammed on his brakes, music still blaring.

"What the hell do you think you're doing?" he bellowed, throwing open his door.

"Stop this!" I screamed back. "They're not zombies! Those are real people!"

"They're not nothing no more!" He stood up on his running board and raised his rifle. "Now get back inside before I decide you're infected too!"

"Mom!" Hillary's voice cracked with fear.

"Get back in the house," I ordered, not taking my eyes off Clyde. "All of you. Now."

"But—" Taylor started.

"Now!"

I heard their feet on the gravel, retreating. I dared a glance over my shoulder. They were halfway to the house, Hillary dragging a reluctant Zeus. Good girls.

"You too," Clyde growled. "Get inside."

"No." I took a step forward, both hands wrapped around the end of my bat. "This ends now."

He laughed, but there was no humor in it. "And how exactly are you going to stop me?"

"By telling you the truth," I said, taking another step. "Every person you've shot might have gotten better. Including Bernadette."

Clyde's finger tightened on the trigger. "Don't you say her name!"

"She might have survived," I pressed on. "Just like James did. Just like all of those people are doing." I gestured toward the figures still stumbling up the ditch. "Look at them, Clyde! Really look! They're not attacking anyone. They're just confused and scared."

"Shut up!"

"You killed her before she had a chance!" The words burst out of me. "You were so scared and angry that you killed your wife before she could get better!"

"She wasn't my wife anymore!" he screamed. "She tried to kill me! She wasn't Bernadette anymore!"

"But she could have been!" I was close enough now to see the tears streaming down his face. "She could have come back to you, just like James came back to Eileen!"

"No!" He swung the rifle toward me. "You're lying! They're dead and they can't get better! You're just a god-damn liar."

"Look at them," I said fiercely. "Really look."

Clyde's head turned slightly and I leaped from the top of the retaining wall to the hood of his pickup truck, baseball bat swinging. Unfortunately, Clyde was still mostly pro-tected by the truck's door, so all I did was make him mad.

"You bitch!" he screamed.

The good news was that my swing had pushed the barrel of his big gun up so he couldn't immediately shoot me.

The bad news was that he really, really wanted to.

32

Wednesday Dusk

Untangling himself from the truck door, Clyde turned toward the back of the truck and wrapped a hand around the chrome pipes protruding from the cab. He swung himself up and into the bed, causing the whole vehicle to rock. The hood swayed beneath my feet and I widened my stance. Through it all Lynyrd Skynyrd crooned from the speakers at stadium volume.

"Mom!" Frances's voice cut through the song's chorus.

"Keep everyone inside!" I yelled without moving my gaze from Clyde.

He stood in the center of the pickup's bed, with his back to me.

Before him the growing horde of infected clogged the ditch. The music was agitating them, as designed. They were all focused on Clyde, standing above them with his rifle.

The sun had sunk over the top of the mountain and the only light back here was from the big floodlights installed on the truck. They cast the gaunt features of the infected into high relief, turning their faces into death heads with red eyes and gaping mouths.

They looked like zombies.

I knew that's what Clyde was seeing, but I'd seen James. I'd seen Mark.

"They're not dead," I screamed over the music. "They're just sick. And dehydrated." I braced my free hand on the cab of the truck, desperate to reach him.

"This isn't a movie, Clyde. Zombies aren't real. These people are real, they're just sick," I repeated.

He looked back at me over his shoulder, his expression flat. "You want me to ignore what I'm seeing with my own eyes. You want me to be the villain, but I'm the hero."

"Jane!" That was Hector's voice.

Behind Clyde, more and more infected were arriving, drawn by the music. There were dozens, pushing each other against the back of the truck. Hands pawed at the tailgate, fingers clawing over the top edge. Someone must have gotten lucky, because the gate fell open.

"Get back!" Clyde yelled.

He aimed the rifle into the crowd and fired. The shot rang out as the infected surged over the top of the open tailgate.

"That's my mom!" Taylor's voice cracked. "Don't shoot my mom!"

I planted a sneaker on the top of the cab and surged up and over. My bat was already swinging as the bed of the truck rushed up at me. The thickest part of the bat landed across Clyde's shoulders and a vibration ran up the wood shaft and into my arms a second before my feet hit the bed. My fingers were numb but I didn't let go. It wasn't just my life that depended on it.

I guess I've led a sheltered existence, because I don't think I've ever been in the back of a pickup truck before—or at least not since I was a little kid. The bottom of the truck wasn't flat. The metal was wavy, like a piece of corrugated cardboard, and the width of each rut was narrower than my foot, but not narrow enough to step on two at a time. It was an awkward surface to land on and I nearly went right over. I had to brace my knees and just let my ankle flex so that my foot was wedged at an angle into the gap. But that gave me a little extra leverage.

I used that leverage to pull back the bat for another swing as Clyde turned toward me, his back rounded and his face twisted in rage. The barrel of the rifle was moving down toward me and his mouth was open in a snarl.

The damn music was still playing in the background, nearly drowning out the screams of the girls, Hector crying my name again, and the moans of the infected. The flood lights mounted on the back of the cab behind me reflected off each of Clyde's teeth but the interior of his mouth was a black pit. His head reared back, giving me an up-the-nose view as his eyes narrowed to slits.

I brought the bat around with all of my strength, pushing off against where my feet were braced into the bed of the truck. The crack of the wood bat against the barrel of Clyde's gun cut through all of the noise, ringing across the top of the mountain.

The gun flew away from Clyde's hands and tumbled over his shoulder. It spun end over end toward the horde of infected clambering at the tailgate of the truck.

Clyde lunged after it.

An emaciated man wearing the remnants of a flannel shirt had just managed to hoist himself over the edge of the tailgate when Clyde's outstretched arm passed over his head. Eyes red and face contorted with pain or rage, the infected grabbed Clyde's arm and they both tumbled backwards into the mob.

"Holy crap," I whispered, shocked.

There was no sign of Clyde. He was just gone.

The crowd of infected were a mass of moving body parts, red eyes, and grasping hands. Another figure pulled itself over the tailgate and I jolted, stumbling backward on the uneven surface. Time to go.

"Jane!" Hector was standing on the retaining wall, hands outstretched toward me.

I braced one foot on the side of the truck and leaped toward him without a second thought. My body crashed into his as his arms wrapped around me and we both went tumbling to the soft grass.

33

Thursday

The music died just after midnight. Yes, we were all still awake, but no one went to check. I sent the girls to bed.

It was dawn by the time I worked up the nerve to go back out there, Zeus on my heels.

Clyde's truck sat exactly where he'd left it, but the infected had dispersed sometime during the night, no doubt wandering back down the ditch and into the town and surrounding countryside.

There was no sign of Clyde.

I walked back into the house with Zeus by my side and started the coffee, watching the colors paint the sky.

Behind me, the house was beginning to stir. Lucy was the first one up, as usual. She padded into the kitchen and grabbed two mugs from the cabinet.

"All quiet?" she asked softly.

I shrugged. "So far."

She poured the coffee and came to stand beside me. "Do you think he's..."

"I don't know." I accepted the mug and took a sip. "I couldn't see anything last night and there's no sign of him this morning."

Hillary stumbled into the kitchen, her hair a rat's nest. "I need hot chocolate."

Ivy was right behind her, with a hopeful expression. "We have hot chocolate?"

"Nope. How about warm goat's milk with honey?" Lucy offered.

Hillary considered this. "Deal."

"Me too," Ivy chimed in, looking only slightly less excited.

Lucy smiled and went to heat the milk.

Hillary plopped down into one of the chairs and laid her head on the table. "So, do we think Clyde is dead?"

"Hillary!" I gasped. "Geez."

"What? It's a valid question."

I sat beside her at the table and sighed. She wasn't wrong.

"I don't know," I admitted again.

Hillary lifted her head to peer at me through her hair. "But like, probably dead, right?"

Frances appeared in the doorway, Taylor right behind her. They both looked like they hadn't slept.

"Any sign of my parents?" Taylor asked.

I shook my head. "It looks like the infected all moved back down the mountain."

Taylor's face crumpled and Frances wrapped an arm around her shoulders. "We'll look for them," she promised.

"I want to go now," Taylor said.

"In a couple of hours," I said firmly. "It will get a little warmer. And we can ask Hector to go with us."

Hillary perked up when Lucy set two mugs of warm milk down on the table. "Let's go check on our last batch of cheese."

Lucy's eyes lit up. "Ooh, yes! It's been long enough."

Hillary downed her milk like a shot of whisky, slamming the empty glass on the table with an inappropriate amount of force. She disappeared into the basement with Lucy before I worked up the energy to complain. Ivy sat with us for a while and savored her milk, then headed back upstairs with Frances and Taylor to plan their search party. I stayed by the window, watching the path down the mountain.

When Hector finally appeared on the road, something in my chest loosened.

I met him on the porch.

"Any sign of Clyde?" he asked, reaching for my hand.

I shook my head. "Nothing. Not even the rifle."

His fingers intertwined with mine, warm and solid. "How are you doing this morning?"

His gaze ran over my face, but my eyes were dry. And they had been all night. I may not be exactly well-rested, but I had slept.

"I'm okay," I said honestly. "Not great, but okay."

"You did what you had to do," Hector said firmly, stepping closer.

"I know," I told him, letting my free hand come to rest on his chest as if it were the most natural thing in the world. "I swear, I really am okay."

Hector's gaze searched my face. "I know how hard it was for you after Tom—"

"I didn't know that Tom could be saved," I started, taking a deep breath. "But even if I did, it all happened so fast. I accept that I couldn't have done anything differently." I gave a small smile. "At least nothing that wouldn't have ended up with me dead."

Hector closed the remaining distance between us. "I am so very, very glad that you aren't dead."

I gave a little laugh, resting my head on his shoulder. "I'm really glad that you're not dead, too."

"There were a lot of people I couldn't save," he whispered.

I lifted my head and met his warm, dark gaze, his face inches from mine. "You saved me."

"You saved yourself," he corrected. "I just helped a little at the end."

"A lot," I argued, and then his lips were on mine and I forgot what we were talking about.

The kiss was gentle at first, almost hesitant. But then his hand slid into my hair and I pressed closer, wanting more. He tasted like coffee and something sweet, and I couldn't get enough.

"Guys!" Hillary's voice shattered the moment. "Mom's kissing Hector!"

We broke apart, laughing.

"Way to ruin the moment, kid," I called over my shoulder.

"That's what I do best!" She grinned at us through the screen door. "Also, Lucy says to come quick because the cheese is doing something weird."

I groaned. "Oh, great."

Hector caught my hand as I turned to go inside. "We'll continue this later?"

"Definitely," I promised.

Inside, the kitchen was chaos, but Lucy and Hillary were both beaming with pride.

"We did it!" Hillary announced. "Real cheese!"

"Sort of," Lucy amended. "It's like cottage cheese, but not really. It's cheese-adjacent."

"It's progress," I agreed, surveying the concoction.

"Are we sure that's edible?" Ivy asked. "Someone else can go first."

Zeus whined and flopped down under the table.

"Cowards," Hillary declared.

34

One Week Later

Taylor

Taylor sat on the front porch steps, scrolling through updates on her phone. The signal was still weak, but at least they didn't have to climb onto the roof anymore to check for messages. She checked everyone's entries to see if there were any new notes. Hector had left messages for several friends and Ryan had left messages for his wife and a bunch of family members. Jane had even left one for her ex-husband, which Taylor thought was nice.

Taylor smiled as she passed the green check beside Ivy's entry. Her mom had never been infected, it turned out. She'd been trapped in her office for days and then couldn't reach Ivy with the phone lines down. She'd shown up at the gate hours after they'd added their info to the database and Ivy was home now.

Her thumb paused over the survivor database entry she'd created for her parents. No replies yet, but people were being found every day as more and more of the infected recovered. There were hundreds of thousands of unidentified people in medical centers all over the country.

The screen door creaked open behind her and Lucy emerged with two steaming mugs. "Tea?" she offered, settling beside Taylor on the step.

"Thanks." Taylor accepted the mug, wrapping both hands around its warmth.

The mornings were getting cooler.

"Any word on when we might get power back?" Lucy asked.

Taylor shook her head. "They're prioritizing the cities and main roads first. Jane says it could be months."

"Makes sense, I guess." Lucy took a careful sip of tea.

"Have you decided what you're going to do?" Taylor asked.

"I think so." Lucy's fingers drummed against her mug. "It looks like I can go back to school as soon as campus re-opens." She smiled over the rim as she took a sip. "Seems like this semester is a complete do-over. I picked a really good time to go off the rails."

"How convenient," Taylor smiled at her friend.

Behind them, Hillary's voice drifted through the screen door, complaining loudly about the inevitability of returning to school in the spring.

"I don't see why we have to go back," Hillary whined. "We learned plenty during the apocalypse. Like cheese-making and chicken handling."

"I don't think those are on the standard curriculum," Jane responded dryly.

Lucy laughed softly. "I'm going to miss this place."

"You'll visit though, right?" Taylor asked. "For holidays and stuff?"

"Yup, Jane already made me promise." Lucy bumped her shoulder against Taylor's. "Besides, someone has to make sure Hillary doesn't poison everyone with her culinary experiments."

They sat in silence for a while, watching the morning mist rise from the valley below.

Taylor's thoughts drifted to her parents, as they often did. Search parties were still looking for people who had wandered off into the forest, but they were coming back with fewer and fewer survivors every day. They were still finding plenty of bodies. She wasn't sure if that was better or worse than not knowing.

"I keep thinking about that night," Taylor said quietly. "I swear I saw them in the crowd."

Lucy nodded. "Even if they were there, that doesn't mean—"

"I know." Taylor wiped at her eyes. "The recovery rate is really high. I just wish..." She let the thought trail off.

"Hey." Lucy wrapped an arm around her shoulders. "Don't give up hope. More people are being found every day."

Taylor's phone buzzed in her lap and she nearly dropped it in surprise. An unknown number flashed across the screen.

"Hello?" she answered hesitantly.

"Taylor?" Her mother's voice crackled through the speaker. "Baby, is that you?"

Taylor's hand flew to her mouth as tears sprang to her eyes. "Mom?"

"Oh, thank god." Her mother's voice broke. "I can't believe we found you. The phones are so unreliable..."

"We?" Taylor could barely breathe. "Is Dad..."

"I'm here, princess." Her father's voice joined in, slightly distant as if he were leaning toward the phone. "We're both here."

Lucy squeezed Taylor's shoulders as she began to sob.

"Where are you? Are you okay?" Taylor choked out, trying to breathe.

"We're at the medical center in Richmond," her mother explained. "We've been here a couple of days, but we've been on the waiting list for the phone. Everyone is in the same boat."

"You're really okay?" Taylor managed between hiccups.

"We are now," her father assured her. "The doctors say we're expected to make a full recovery. No lasting effects."

"When can I see you?" The words tumbled out. "Can I come to Richmond?"

There was a pause and some murmuring in the background.

"Where are you now?" her mother asked. "Are you safe where you are?"

"I'm at Frances's house. The Kovaks? You remember Frances from school?" Taylor wiped her face with her sleeve. "I'm safe here."

"Oh, baby." Her mother's voice was thick with tears. "I'm so glad you're okay."

Lucy quietly stood and slipped inside, giving Taylor privacy for the conversation.

"Can you stay there for a little longer?" her father asked. "It's not completely safe here yet. But they should release us in a couple of days and we'll figure out how to get to you."

"Okay," Taylor agreed. "Take your time, just get better. We're all okay here. We even figured out how to make cheese."

Her mother laughed, the sound so wonderfully familiar it made her chest ache.

There was murmuring in the background.

"Someone else needs to use the phone now," her mother explained, "but we'll see you soon. We both love you so much."

"I love you, too!" Taylor clutched the phone to her chest long after the line was dead, happy tears streaming down her face.

When her heartbeat had slowed down, she wiped her cheeks and ran into the house, nearly taking the door off its hinges in her excitement.

"Jane!"

She appeared in the kitchen doorway, covered in flour. Hillary peered around her, face also dusted white.

"What's wrong? Lucy said you got a call?" Jane asked, wiping her hands on a tea towel.

"My parents!" Taylor waved the phone toward them. "They're okay! They're in Richmond!"

Jane's face split into a brilliant smile. "Oh, thank god!" She wrapped Taylor in a fierce hug, getting flour all over both of them. "Oh honey, I'm so happy for you."

Taylor buried her face in Jane's shoulder for a moment, breathing in the familiar scent of coffee and fresh bread. When she looked up, she found the entire household had gathered in the kitchen. Frances immediately pulled her into a hug while Hillary bounced excitedly beside them.

"See?" Hillary declared. "This is way better than school! Real-life happy endings!"

"It's not an ending," Lucy corrected gently.

Hillary clapped her hands, sending a cloud of flour into the air. "This calls for celebratory cheese!"

"No!" everyone shouted in unison.

"You guys are no fun," Hillary pouted.

Taylor laughed, joy bubbling up inside her like champagne. Her parents were alive. They were okay. And somehow, impossibly, she had ended up with two families instead of none.

"Maybe we could just make regular food?" she suggested. "You know, the kind that doesn't require hazmat suits to prepare?"

"Boring," Hillary declared, but she was grinning. "Fine. But I'll make something awesome for dessert."

"God help us all," Jane muttered, but she was smiling too.

35
Thanksgiving

Frances and Taylor chatted non-stop in the backseat, their voices rising and falling like music. I kept my eyes on the road, carefully navigating around the occasional pile or debris or charred spot.

"It's looking better," Hector observed.

"Still a long way to go, though," I muttered, steering around a ring of traffic cones standing guard over a very suspicious crater in the middle of main street. The road crews had been working for weeks, but there was still so much to clear.

Honestly, though, the town looked a lot better than the last time I'd seen it. No more cars crashed into the side of buildings, although there was still a lot of damage and some buildings had just burned all the way to the ground. Taylor's house was on a street that seemed to have fared better than most. All of the houses were still standing, at least.

Taylor practically vibrated out of her seat as we approached the house. "That one!" She pointed toward two figures standing by the door. "That's them. They're here!"

I barely had time to put the car in park before Taylor was out the door, running toward her parents. Frances jumped out after her, but Hector and I followed more slowly, giving them space for their reunion.

Taylor crashed into her parents, all three of them crying.

As we approached, Taylor began talking a mile a minute, telling her parents about everything they'd missed. Her mother looked tired but happy, only a slight tremor in her hands betraying any lasting effects of the infection. Her father's arm was in a sling, but his smile was bright as he held his daughter close with his good arm.

Taylor's mother looked up, tears streaming down her face. "You must be Frances. Oh honey, thank you for taking care of our girl."

Frances shuffled her feet, uncomfortable with the praise. "It was my mom, really."

Taylor's mom shook her head and pulled Frances into a fierce hug. "Thank you," she whispered. "Thank you for being her family when we couldn't."

Taylor's dad turned to smile at me over his daughter's head, eyes glistening. "We can never repay you."

I shook my head. "We were lucky to have her. She helped keep Frances grounded through everything." I smiled at the girls. "They helped each other."

The goodbyes were tearful, with promises to visit soon and stay in touch. Frances and Taylor hugged for a long time, whispering together. Finally, the three of us got back in the car and I watched in the rearview mirror as Taylor waved until we turned the corner.

Frances was quiet as we drove through the city. I glanced back to find her staring out the window, lost in thought.

"You okay, sweetie?"

She nodded. "Yeah. I'm really happy for Taylor. But I'm going to miss her."

"I know." I reached back and squeezed her knee. "But she's not that far away. And you'll see her at school soon."

"I guess that's the bright side of school starting again." Frances managed a small smile. "Grocery store?"

"Absolutely." I pulled into the newly reopened grocery store, marveling at how normal everything looked. The parking lot was half full, the lights were on, and people were going about their business as if the world hadn't nearly ended.

Inside, the shelves were stocked with the staples, though there were still plenty of gaps. We stuck together, going down each aisle. I never thought I'd be so excited about generic, single-ply toilet paper. Frances grabbed baking supplies and Hector hefted a large bag of dog food into our cart. At the front of the store, a woman just waved us past when I tried to pay.

The drive home was peaceful, Frances chattering in the backseat about cooking and school. About halfway up the mountain, I spotted an unfamiliar pickup truck in the distance.

As we passed the last corner I saw the vehicle slow and come to a stop in front of Luis's house. A blonde woman jumped down from the cab as Ryan emerged from the house, Joey in his arms. The woman stumbled slightly, then caught herself and ran toward them.

"Oh my god," Frances breathed. "Is that...?"

"Amber," Hector finished.

Tears immediately flooded my eyes as Ryan's wife pulled herself to stop before her husband and son. Luis appeared at Ryan's shoulder, pulling Joey from his father's frozen arms. As if a switch were flipped, Ryan closed the distance to Amber, wrapping her in his arms.

I stopped the car in front of the gate as Amber pulled back from Ryan's embrace. She looked past him and Joey squirmed to be put down. Luis sat him gently on the ground and he toddled toward his mother, who scooped him up, covering his face with kisses.

"Another happy ending," Frances said softly.

"Another happy beginning," I corrected, wiping the tears from my face. "Go ahead," I told Hector. "I need to get these groceries inside before Hillary decides to make more cheese."

He laughed and leaned over to kiss my cheek. "The last batch was almost edible."

"*Almost* being the key word," I pointed out. "If Amber is up for it, we'd love to have everyone for dinner tonight."

As soon as Luis had helped Hector unload their groceries, I continued up the road to our house and pulled into the driveway. I was still smiling as Frances and I walked into the kitchen carrying our supplies. Lucy and Hillary were sitting at the table with a deck of cards.

"Guess who just rolled up to Luis's house?" Frances asked, vibrating with excitement. "It's Joey's mom!" she answered before either girl could open their mouths.

"Oh, no!" Hillary wailed, jumping up from the table and sprinting for the door. "She's going to take Joey away!"

"Hillary!" I called after her. "Wait!" I threw my hands in the air. "Frances, go after your sister and make sure she doesn't do anything too weird. I'll put the groceries away and be right there."

"I'll help you," Lucy laughed.

Together we made quick work of putting everything away.

"I'm so happy for Ryan and Joey," Lucy sighed. "I'll miss them, though."

"I know." My smile faded just a bit. It was getting to be time for everyone to go back to their lives.

36

Christmas Morning

The world was quieter than usual. The quality of light filtering through the curtains was different too—softer, whiter. I slipped out from under Hector's arm and padded to the window, drawing back the curtain.

My breath caught. The mountain was transformed, draped in pristine white. Fat snowflakes drifted lazily past the window, adding to the blanket that already covered everything. It was the kind of perfect, magical snow that usually only exists in Christmas movies.

Behind me, Hector stirred. "Come back to bed," he mumbled. "It's cold."

I smiled, letting the curtain fall back into place. "It snowed."

"Mmm." He opened one eye. "First snow of the season?"

"First snow on the mountain for me." I climbed back into bed and he pulled me close, his warmth immediately chasing away the chill. "Merry Christmas."

"Merry Christmas," he murmured into my hair.

I snuggled closer, grateful for his solid presence. We never did find out what happened to my ex or his secretary in Paris. They were among the thousands still listed as missing, presumed dead. I'd stopped checking the survivor database. Whatever had happened to them, that chapter of my life was closed.

Hector's phone buzzed on the nightstand. He reached for it with a groan. "It's Ted."

"Tell him Merry Christmas."

"He says congratulations on my 'demotion to Mayberry.'" Hector chuckled as he typed a response. "I told him solving chicken theft cases is very fulfilling work."

"Hey, those were important chickens." I poked him in the ribs. "And technically they weren't stolen, they just wandered through the fence."

"Details, details." He set the phone aside and pulled me closer. "I love it here."

"Me too." I traced my fingers along his arm.

The scratch of claws on the hardwood floor interrupted us, followed by the click of Hillary's door opening. Footsteps padded down the hall as Hillary led Zeus downstairs to go outside.

We waited.

"Three... two... one..." Hector counted down.

Right on cue, Hillary's shriek of joy pierced the morning quiet. "It's snowing!"

I laughed. "We should probably get up before she drags everyone outside in their pajamas."

"Probably," Hector agreed, but neither of us moved.

Down the hall, Frances's door opened. "It's too early for this much enthusiasm," she grumbled.

"Frances, Lucy, it's snowing!" Hillary's voice carried clearly through the house. "Come on, Zeus needs to go out anyway. You can help me build a snowman!"

"Fine," Frances sighed, but I could hear the smile in her voice. "Let me get my boots."

I closed my eyes, soaking in the moment. The quiet of the snow outside, the warmth of the man beside me, the sounds of the girls getting ready for a snow day. Even Zeus's excited barking as Hillary let him out into the fresh powder felt perfect.

"We should join them," Hector whispered against my ear.

"In a minute," I replied and settled back against him. "Let's just stay here a little while longer."

I smiled as Hector's arms tightened around me, listening to the sounds of my family enjoying the snow. There would be time later for snowmen and hot chocolate, for Christmas presents and dinner gathered around the table. For now, I was content just to be here, safe and warm, surrounded by love.

Who knew the apocalypse could have such a happy ending?

About the Author

Mary Jane Owen is a pseudonym for Ms. Michael Owens, whose parents should never be allowed to name anything. An artist, teacher, single mother, and certified Crazy Dog Lady, Michael took an early retirement during the pandemic to write books in an old yellow farmhouse near the sea.

You can find more books by Michael at http://pepper backpress.com.

More by Mary Jane Owen

Blast from the Past

Anne Welsh is a typical single mom...until she stumbles into a bank robbery and is outed as missing CIA agent Trixie Bigotti.

After thirteen peaceful years in suburbia, Trixie finds herself on the run with her teenage daughter. Between dodging aging mobsters and bumbling assassins, she has to come clean about her identity with the people who matter most.

FBI Agent Jay Stowe was madly in love with Trixie before her suspicious death and has carried a torch for her all of these years. When the love of his life pops back up—with a daughter who has his eyes—Jay is ALL IN.

It's time for this secret agent turned soccer mom to solve the mysteries of her past and protect her future from the dangers that surround her. Along the way she just may discover that she was never as alone as she thought she was.

Available wherever books are sold.

https://amazon.com/dp/B0B3S37QQT

What Goes Around

Trixie Bigotti is back and feeling good!

The bad guys are defeated and she's enjoying some quality time with a certain FBI Special Agent...

Codename: Hot Stuff.

It's been two months since Trixie put her past to bed and things are finally getting back to normal. She has a shiny new driver's license with her real name and she's not hiding from anything or anyone...except maybe commitment.

And men with machine guns.

Despite her best efforts, Trixie and the people she loves are once again at the center of a storm of trouble. The difference is, this time Trixie knows that she has help in her corner.

Trixie Bigotti may not be a secret agent anymore, but she's still got a few tricks up her sleeve. The bad guys who brought trouble to her little neck of the woods are about to have a serious case of regret.

Available wherever books are sold.

https://amazon.com/dp/B0DQYDRW8J

Want more?
@pepperbackpress

www.ingramcontent.com/pod-product-compliance
Lightning Source LLC
Chambersburg PA
CBHW061644190726
48289CB00006B/1736